NIGHT COVER
"In the several days during w his long waking hours, Leroy alive."
The New Yorker

CALLED BY A PANTHER (Winner of a "Marlowe" in Germany)
"…so amusing, the wonder is that it also works so well as a thriller… Fast, funny and brilliant."
Tom Nolan, *The Wall Street Journal*

HARD LINE ('82 winner of the "Falcon" in Japan)
"Tersely written, with particularly effective dialogue."
Newgate Callendar, *The New York Times*

"…expertly cross-plotted, and viciously funny."
Kirkus

MISSING WOMAN (Adapted for television in Japan)
"Sharp style, crisp dialogue, believable characters."
***New York Times Book Review* Critic's Choice for 1981**

OUTSIDE IN
"An absolutely first rate story."
Robin Winks, *The New Republic*

AND BABY WILL FALL (Adapted for television in Japan.)
"Adele Buffington… conducts herself like a *mensch*. She shows courage… [and] uses her brains and initiative…"
Marilyn Stasio, *The New York Times*

THE SILENT SALESMAN
"It's superb entertainment."
Earl Waters, Chattanooga Times

ROVER'S TALES

"There's something genuinely moving here... I often found my eyes tearing."

David Nicholson, *The Washington Post*

FAMILY PLANNING

"Mordantly funny, beguiling in the extreme."

Booklist

ASK THE RIGHT QUESTION (Edgar nominee)

"...one of those... books that leads you to shut off the TV and enjoy reading again."

Rick Goodwin, *The News-Sun, Waukegan*

THE RELUCTANT DETECTIVE (includes 2 Edgar nominations)

"...excellent non-series stories and two treats: ... 'Danny' Quayle stories featuring our former Vice President."

Jeff Meyerson, *CADS*

FAMILY BUSINESS

"Totally beguiling, with the lightest of dry touches."

John Coleman, *The Sunday Times* (London)

CONFESSIONS OF A DISCONTENTED DEITY

"Confessions is a joy and I'm sure it will entertain everyone lucky enough to read it, bishops, priests and born-again Christians included. Rabbis too. There's such good sense and wisdom at the heart of this wonderful romp through heaven and earth. The brilliance is that while we are treated to such fun with a God learning to be streetwise, the story is rooted in good theology. I hope He will return."

Peter Lovesey, Grand Master of Mystery Writers of America; Diamond Dagger winner of the Crime Writers Association

Whatever It Takes

Michael Z Lewin

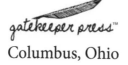

gatekeeper press™
Columbus, Ohio

Whatever It Takes

Published by Gatekeeper Press
2167 Stringtown Rd, Suite 109
Columbus, OH 43123-2989
www.GatekeeperPress.com

The cover design and editorial work for this book are entirely the product of the author. Gatekeeper Press did not participate in and is not responsible for any aspect of these elements.

Cover design Sam Camden-Smith

"The Favor" appeared in the Jan/Feb 2022 issue of Ellery Queen Mystery Magazine

ISBN (paperback): 9781662913143
eISBN: 9781662913150

CONTENTS

For Liz, Roger, Aimee, Simon, Julie, Pansy Valiant, and Liza.

Memories matter.

Whatever
It Takes

1. THE FAVOR

The old man stood outside the grocery – one of the last in the city that opened into the evening. His arms were folded across his chest and he was shivering. The weather was on the turn and not for the better. The difficulties of caring for his little family could only get worse.

He looked up and down the street. It was nearly nine-fifteen and the flickering streetlight couldn't compete with the dark. Nobody came by.

As he shivered he glanced at the window behind him. Posters advertized frozen peas, cereal and toilet paper. Something for everyone? But there were no gaps; he couldn't see inside.

Then a tall man approached – perhaps in his mid-twenties. The old man stepped away from the window and shuffled toward the grocery's door. Was the young man planning to shop?

He wasn't. He walked past, barely noticing the shivering figure whose flannel shirt wasn't heavy enough for the chilly evening.

Well, of course the guy wasn't going in: he wasn't wearing a mask.

A few minutes later two maskless girls came by. Again the old man moved in front of the grocery door but he wasn't surprised when they passed without any interruption to their laughing conversation. He did look after them – it had been so long since he'd heard strangers who sounded happy.

With the sidewalk empty again, he checked the window on the other side of the door. Posters there offered specials on beer and there was an old-fashioned neon sign that had once blazed "liquor" but, like the streetlight, it was on the blink.

Nothing to be seen inside, the old man leaned on the window as if he could absorb some heat from the lighted glass.

The next passers-by were a man and his dog – neither masked: again obviously not shoppers.

A rusty taxi drove by, the first motor vehicle since he'd begun waiting. This was the busiest street the old man had been on in ages.

Then a pickup stopped on the opposite side of the street in front of the closed businesses there – a florist and a funeral parlor. A chunky guy in a black leather jacket jumped down from the cab and crossed toward the old man, who was now trying to rub some warmth into his hands. As the younger man drew near he pulled a mask from a pocket.

The old man straightened himself and moved to block the grocery door. "Excuse me," he said.

Leather Jacket, in his thirties, stopped half a dozen feet from the old man, clearly surprised both by being obstructed and by being spoken to. After a moment he said, "Yeah?"

"Are you going into the store?"

He waved his mask. "You got a problem with that?"

"None at all, none at all. It's just, well…"

"What?" Leather Jacket asked, impatient but also with a hint of sympathy. This was an old guy – maybe Leather Jacket had a grandfather of his own who he loved. Or had loved.

"I was hoping you'd do me a favor," the old man said.

"What kind of favor?"

"See, I came out in a hurry, because I knew this store was gonna close soon, yeah?"

Leather Jacket looked at his phone. "At nine-thirty? Or does it stay open till ten?"

"Nine-thirty," the old man said, gesturing to one of the signs that plastered the entry door. "So I was in a hurry, and I come out without a mask. And you need a mask to buy stuff in there nowadays, see?"

Leather Jacket again held up the mask he was carrying. "I'm not going to lend it to you."

"No no, and I wouldn't take it. Who knows what you got. And I'm old, and…" He coughed. "I got these lungs, see."

"So…?"

"I really want a six-pack. I opened the fridge and, hell, I was all out. I didn't keep track. So I looked at the clock – I got this nice clock on the sill that they gave me for forty years and it said I was nearly too late. So I rushed out." He held up a wallet. "I got the money. Not looking for a handout. But I forgot my jacket." He demonstrated cold by hugging himself. "Mask in the pocket, see? No time to go back, so I need some help."

Leather Jacket smiled, even gave a little laugh. "Yeah, I'll get you a six-pack. What kind you want?"

"Damnedest thing, ain't it," the old man said. "Sixty years ago I stood outside this same store – well not *this* store, but one like it. I lived somewhere completely different. Well, not so different – same kind of neighborhood. So many neighborhoods have changed in all that time, but not this one. Lots of different people, getting along." A nod, "And helping each other."

Leather Jacket shrugged.

"So there I was, sixty years ago, fourteen years-old, and I was outside the store asking a stranger to get me a six-pack – any kind of six-pack, like today, any kind, thanks – because I was too young. I had fake ID, but the people who owned the store, they knew my auntie – she and her fella was the ones raised me up – and they knew how old I wasn't. So I had to get someone to buy the beer *for* me, see. Didn't have to be a stranger – like you – because sometimes one of the older kids in the neighborhood would do it. Y'know how kids are, eh.

When they're young they want to be older but, wait till they're as old as me. All us kids in the neighborhood wanted to drink beer. Wine wasn't so common in those days and we never got a crack at whisky or anything like that. But that night, I remember, I had me a girl – a girlfriend pretty much – and she was hoping I'd get some beer, and I was hoping too, you know? I expect a good looking guy like you doesn't have any problems that way, and I didn't either later on, but then I was fourteen, like I said, and she was older. Fifteen. And she was payin' me attention – you know? Kissing me and that. And if I could score some beer, who knew? So I was standing outside a store – not this one, but one like it – and I was asking people to get me a six-pack. I had the money. Not enough for a carton. And it wasn't late, like tonight. Stores closed earlier back in the day. I don't remember exactly, but probably they closed at six, these friends of my auntie. My mom and dad, well, my dad took a hike after my little sister, Plum, was born, and then my mom died in a crash with Plum – hit and run – and my auntie took me in. And it was OK, even when she hooked up with this new guy and he, Charlie, he didn't mind me as long as I kept out of the way, you know, and—"

"Look, old timer, it's getting late." Leather Jacket held up his phone. "Tick-tock. You want this beer or not?"

"Oh I do, I do. I could kill for a beer. Or some wine – it's red I like, though I can't tell much difference one

5

from another for the ones I can afford." The old man opened his wallet and began to look for money. "It's in here, it's in here. I know it's in here."

Suddenly behind him the grocery door opened. A tall, lean boy emerged followed by a much shorter woman. Both wore black balaclavas – not masks – and they carried plastic bags. And handguns. The boy pushed the old man aside, but not roughly.

Leather Jacket gaped, then took a step back, hands raised.

The boy said, "Let's go, Grandpa. We're done."

The old man's voice became instantly stronger. "Hurt anyone?"

"No need. The guy was angry and told us how crazy we were but he folded when I waved the gun in his face." The boy passed between the old man and Leather Jacket.

The woman took the old man's elbow as she followed. "He did fine, Pa. C'mon, let's get out of here."

"I'm coming."

Leather Jacket still had his hands in the air as the old man headed for the darkness, saying, "See? It's me done you the favor this time. You can thank me later."

2. SOMETHIN' TO SAY?

The old man sat on the floor with his back against a wall. "Y'know," he said, "that richie I was talking to last night. He had this great leather jacket."

"Yeah?" His grandson sat facing a row of cans. They were lit by a candle.

"Black. Not too new, not too old. I bet it was about my size."

The boy gave a quiet snort.

"What?"

"Nothing, Grandpa."

"Nothing? I know nothing and that wasn't nothing. Didn't you see the jacket? I bet your Ma did. Or do you think it wasn't my size? Your Ma would know. Got a good eye, your Ma."

The boy looked up from studying the stolen canned goods. "Why're you thinking about a jacket you're never going to see again?"

"You never know."

"Yeah, you never know." Another snort. "Sorry, Grandpa. Maybe I'm getting a cold." He stifled a chuckle.

"Just make sure it's into your krelbow if you gotta cough. Don't want you spreading germs from your hands on stuff. You don't know who touched those cans before you."

"I wiped them, Grandpa. And I'm washing my hands like Ma told me when she left me to sort them out." The boy held a can close to the candle. He opened it and sniffed.

"What's that? What'd you open?"

"Artichoke hearts. I wondered what they looked like."

"*What* hearts?"

"Artichoke. In spring water. Don't you like artichoke hearts?"

"Don't much like anything that chokes."

Another snort. "Sorry, Grandpa."

"Where is your ma?"

"Foodbank. You were still asleep."

"She went alone?"

"She says sometimes she does better there when she's alone."

"Yeah. But…"

"I offered to go with her but it's the morning and it's sunny. And she said she can take care of herself."

The old man thought about it. His daughter was small but she knew how to fight – he'd made sure of that, back in the day. She could certainly deliver some low blows if she had to. Had she taken one of the guns? Probably not in case she was stopped. He gave his head a shake.

The boy held up another can. "Pork and beans. Hungry?"

That was more like it. But, "Wait till she gets back."

The candle began to gutter. The boy lit another and for a time the light in the room was brighter. But not bright.

They took care about light that might be seen by passers-by in the street. That's how squatting in empty stores worked, although suddenly lots of stores were empty. They still had owners, no matter that they were worthless. Some owners hated their properties being used even by respectful strangers who would do no damage. You heard stories down at the foodbank sometimes.

"That was a good jacket," the old man said. "A real good jacket."

"Yeah?"

"Back in the day, I had me a black leather jacket. Nehru collar, couple of pockets in the lining. I looked good, I tell you now. Not everybody looks good in black leather."

"No?"

"I remember I was in a bar one time. Drinking with my pals – this was before I was married to your Grandma – and they were talking about a kid who was on the fringe of the group, because we were a group back then. Not a gang. Gangs weren't how it worked where I grew up. No tatts, no swearing oaths in blood. None of that. And I was young. Like maybe nineteen, even if my ID said I was twenty-two. I had it say an extra year on it so I wasn't like all the ones who said, 'Yeah, my birthday was yesterday,' y'know? Anyways I was young. And this kid, skinny, blond, face like a piecrust – you know lattice piecrusts? Like that. He had some condition. But he showed up in a brand new black leather jacket and he thought it made him look really tough. Because that's what wearing black leather meant in those days, being tough. This kid, Tony I think his name was, he had a drink with us, showed the jacket off – not prancing around but just making sure we all saw it – and then he went home to momma. And I recall the other guys smiled to each other as he walked out the door and I knew what they were thinking and I said, "Ain't everyone can wear black leather," and I laughed along with them."

The old man paused, nodding to himself. "Yup, I did. But then this other guy, we called him Money, this Money, he turned to me and said, 'You oughta know.' And I said, 'Whatcha mean by that?' And he said, 'You in your poncy collar. What do you think *you* look like?' And the other guys began to laugh because Money, he was kinda, y'know, the big man. It was because he always had money on him and would never tell us where it came from, but money can be worth having. It can make up for a lot. But not for being insulted. So I said to Money, I said, 'You want to come out and say that again,

Mon?' Because I wasn't gonna be talked to like that. I didn't like it. And I stood up. And Money, he looked around to the other guys and I could tell he didn't want to fight me, because he might have had money but it didn't make him tough. Not *really* tough. Black leather's what made you tough in those days. Well, it didn't *make* you tough, it showed you *were* tough. And I tell you, Boy, I was tough in those days. And I'm still no pushover. So I was standing there and I grabbed Money by his shirt and pulled him up to his feet. And I said, 'You got somethin' you want to say to me, Mon? Because you got somethin' to say, you shouldn't hide in here where Alex has a baseball bat behind the bar and isn't afraid to use it if there's a fight. You come outside and say it to me, you got somethin' to say.'"

The old man chuckled to himself. "Somethin' to say," he said. "That's how we put it, back in the day. You lookin' at me? You got somethin' to say?" He chuckled again. "And Money, he put up his hands and he said, 'I didn't mean nothin' by it. I didn't mean nothin'. Like you didn't mean nothin' neither, Boy, I bet. Anyway I just stared hard at Money. And he said, 'We're cool,' and he sat back down. And I said, 'You like my jacket?' And he said, 'Cool jacket, man. Cool.' And I just nodded and sat down too. And he said, 'Let me get you a drink,' and I let him because he'd saved himself a hell of a beating and he knew it. I wouldn't have needed no baseball bat.

That was back in the day when I had me my black leather."

The old man scratched his head. "I don't remember what happened to that jacket. It fit great. Was warm. Had its pockets, y'know." He sat remembering and it was a while before he noticed that the boy had stopped studying the cans and was looking at him. "What?" the old man asked.

"You, Grandpa."

"Me?"

"You never been in a fight in your life, have you?"

The old man was silent for a moment.

"Not one," the boy said. "In your whole life. Ma told me Grandma told her."

After a moment, the old man said, "Maybe not." Then he chuckled, proudly. "But I didn't have to. I heard somewhere – or maybe I read it – 'The best warriors never have to fight.' That's because people know they're gonna get beat. Money, he *knew* I would have whupped him, and whupped him bad. Because that's what black leather does for you, Boy, if you can wear it."

"And that guy last night, Grandpa? Could he wear his black leather?"

The old man chuckled again. "I wouldn't have wanted to fight him, that's for true. No sir, I wouldn't have wanted to. But I would have, for you and your ma, if he'd tried to push past me to interrupt what you were doing."

The boy looked at his grandfather and nodded.

And the old man knew his grandson knew that he'd have done, and would do, whatever it took to keep the remains of his family safe.

3. DOCTORS

The old man woke with a start. "What?" he said. "What?"

"Nothing, Pa," his daughter said. "You were dreaming."

"Was I?" He closed his eyes, tried to remember.

"Twisting and turning. Something was going on in that head of yours."

"Ah," the old man said. "They were after us."

"Who?"

"Men. Maybe some women too. No, men. They had masks. And tubes, tubes like elephants' trunks. Jeez, it was scary." He sat up on his lumpy mattress. "You been to the foodbank?"

"And I made a withdrawal," his daughter said.

In the candlelight the old man could see she was smiling as she sat at the makeshift table sorting cans and packs into piles. He couldn't see what they were. It would be whatever they had in stock to give her at the bank this time. It varied a lot. Where did the stuff come from?

But why was she smiling? Was there something good? He sat up straighter, trying to see better. He felt achy and would prefer to wait a few minutes before rising.

He smoothed a lump out of his sleeping bag where it had bunched up. Princess and the Pea, he thought as he straightened it. Then, why did I think of that? Prince and the Pea? In fact, he had to pee.

He turned, preparing to rise, and felt something on his leg. He jerked away. "What the hell?" Then he saw that it was a tracksuit top and a t-shirt.

"They had clothes this time," his daughter said. "A donation, and because I have 'dependents' so I got some for each of us. They aren't new, but they're clean. They promise they've been decontaminated."

The old man held up the tracksuit top. Navy blue with light blue stripes vertically down the front. A maker's label on the left had been smeared out with a black marker. He held the top up and saw that it would fit. "Thank you," he said. "Looks perfect." Then he examined the t-shirt, black with a star on the front. Below that it said, "Dr. John."

"It's a good weight," his daughter said. "Feel it. People see you in that and they'll say, 'Trust him, he's a doctor.'"

"Doctors give out t-shirts these days?"

A little laugh from his daughter. "You don't know who Dr. John was?" she said, turning to face him more directly. "Oh, right, you never got further than Country, did you?"

The old man felt he was missing something but said, "I haven't known that many doctors. Been lucky that way." He held the shirt up. It *was* a good weight, cotton. And it would fit. A good layer for the coming winter. "A doctor t-shirt? Really?" He looked up at her.

"Try the clothes on, Pa."

"Back in the day doctors would come to your house if you were sick enough, y'know."

"Yeah?" his daughter said, returning to what she'd been doing.

"Maybe that was when all the doctors were men. Not like now. Maybe if the doctor who looked after your mother was a guy it would have worked out different."

"Oh Pa," she said, addressing him again. "You don't really think that, do you?"

"She wasn't supposed to die." He shook his head, but he felt the shaking in his voice and in his guts.

He pictured his wife on a bed, hooked to an oxygen cylinder, but still struggling to breathe. "I asked that doctor we had what I could do to help. Rub her feet or hands or something. Anything, any damn thing. But she said I shouldn't even be there. As if I could be *anywhere* else. Then she read your mother's chest with her stethoscope and stood there shrugging and saying *maybe* she'll be one of the lucky ones." The old man shook his head. "Maybe? Maybe? What's with maybe? They're supposed to know, damnit."

"It wasn't the doctor's fault, Pa. It was the sickness."

The old man looked up at her. "You were there. You saw."

"No, Pa. They wouldn't let me in."

"No," he said, his memory now agreeing with hers. "I remember the first doctor my mother ever took me to. I was having trouble breathing too, y'know."

"Yeah?"

"He heard me breathe and he looked in my nose and he said, 'Is your nose always this blocked up?' Turned out it was allergies and there were pills. But there were no pills for your Ma."

"I miss her too."

"Nowadays doctors don't want to see a poor man."

"No one could have saved her."

"I guess not." Then, "She would have hated all this." He waved vaguely at the dark room.

"She'd hate it," his daughter said, "but she'd be organizing and cleaning and trying to make it brighter, even if we were going to leave tomorrow."

"Yeah," he said. And he pulled himself to his feet, and went to where his daughter sat. He put his arms around her shoulders. "Never liked the dark, y'know, your ma. We always had to have a light on, even if it was just a little one. I used to worry sometimes how much it cost, but I never complained. I could work an extra hour or two."

His daughter stood and they hugged. "Back in the day," she said.

"Back in the day," the old man echoed. "Not that it was all good then."

"No," she said. "But at least we had Ma." She sat again. "Look." Holding up a can in the candlelight. "Corned beef. You like that don't you? I had a good day at the foodbank."

"Bankers," he said, pulling his new jacket on. "You go to them, cap in hand. And if you don't own a cap you borrow one so you can ask to borrow money to buy your own damn cap. They treated you like you were begging on the streets, that's how bad it was."

"A pity begging doesn't work now that there's no one to beg from."

But the old man was adjusting the sleeves and found he had something different on his mind. "Where's the boy?"

"He went out."

"By himself?" The old man settled on a box across from her.

"He's old enough to go out alone."

"On the rob?"

"God no," she said emphatically. "You can't do that without planning it carefully."

"Of course not." The old man thought about it. "I get confused sometimes. Long ago, short ago... I'm sorry I was asleep. Sorry I was dreaming."

"It's living in the dark so much."

"So what *is* he doing?"

"Just looking around. Looking for maybe another empty store, if we need to move quickly."

"He's not happy here?" But the old man laughed before she could reply. "Hell, nobody's *happy* here." But he'd heard something else in her voice. "And…?"

She sighed. "I might have been followed when I left the foodbank."

"Who by?"

"There was this guy outside, thought he was god's gift. Missing a front tooth."

"Did you knock it out?"

"I would have done the other one for him. I *thought* he got the message but something shifty about his eyes made me think maybe he didn't, and that maybe he'd follow me. I didn't come straight here but I couldn't move so fast because of all I was carrying."

"Did you take a gun?"

"Not to the foodbank. It's not like this was an open-carry state. Even back in the day…"

"Maybe I better go out there, look for the boy."

"He'll be OK. He *is* OK. Good head on his shoulders."

"Yeah. But…"

"But what?"

The old man knew what, but he didn't want to say it out loud. He'd lost his wife. Which was just not supposed to happen. She wasn't supposed to die, not then. And it nearly killed him. He wouldn't be able to bear it if something happened to the boy. If he lost *him* too.

If it hadn't been for his daughter, and for the boy… If it hadn't been for all of what was needed now. No telling what he would have done but for them. And he might have taken some doctors, male and female, with him.

But for the moment the thing he need most to do was go out back to pee.

4. THE BIG HOUSE

The old man's daughter held out an artichoke heart on a plastic spoon as the small family sat around the boxes that served as their table. 'G'wan, Pa," she said. "Try one."

The old man's makeshift plate already sported cold Spaghetti-Os, butter beans and corned beef. That was plenty. He waved the spoon away.

The old man's grandson laughed.

"When you was young," the old man said to his daughter, "you wouldn't touch fish. We got some sardines. And snapper soup. Which one would you like me to get for you?"

His daughter popped the spoonful into her own mouth. "This is the kind of snapper I like." She clicked her teeth several times.

The boy laughed again.

His mother nodded toward her son, "Now this one, he'll eat anything."

"Not *any*thing." After a moment, "I don't eat tin cans."

"He's not a goat after all," his mother said to her father. "Who knew?"

After the old man's mother was taken away he'd been fostered by mean people who made him "deserve" every bite of food he got. They told him his mom was bad blood and that she'd left him behind to go to the big house. But there were no big houses in that neighborhood, so he was confused.

"He's got taste," the old man said when he realized the others were looking at him. "He gets that from me."

The boy rubbed his stomach and his mother seemed to be framing a comment when they all heard a noise from the direction of the back door that led to the alley.

The boy jumped up. "They're coming for us. They've come, at last. We gotta run." He turned away from the sound, toward the front of the boarded-up store where another door led to the street.

The adults each took one of the boy's arms. "Wait," the old man said as he blew out the candle on their dining table.

"See what it is," his mother said.

There were more noises. Creakings and bangings but not loud.

"They're not breaking down the door down," the old man said.

He knew what *that* sounded like. The cops who came for his mom when he was six smashed their apartment door to splinters. He hadn't realized how lucky he was before that happened.

A year later she'd come back for him. She was pregnant with Plum and was given an early release because they didn't want her to complain about it. But he never forgot the sound of the door being smashed open. That's not what he was hearing now.

Light was coming through the cracks, so the outside alley door must be open now. His daughter and the boy both held guns. When had they retrieved them from their hiding place?

"Put them guns behind your back," the old man said. "Ready, but not in sight. You don't want to get yourselves killed just because people see you're armed, now do you?"

They hid the weapons.

Then the internal door flew open. The silhouette of one man filled the space. "Fuck," he said, sucking a finger, then a knuckle.

He saw there were people in the room – the old man in front of him and the others either side. "Hi," he said.

The old man said, "Don't take another step if you know what's good for you. Who are you and what do you think you're doing here?"

"I'm Tristan."

"And?"

"And what?"

"What the hell do you want?"

"Oh." Tristan sucked again on his knuckle and then pulled a flashlight from a pants pocket.

"Put that out," the old man said, taking a step toward the intruder.

"Guns?" Tristan said, looking at the woman and the boy. "Shit, no need for that. I don't want to do you any harm. The opposite."

"Give me the flashlight," the old man said.

Tristan held it out and the old man took it. He heard a click – a revolver being cocked, at his daughter's side.

"Jesus, Mary and Joseph," Tristan said. He raised his hands. "No harm. No foul."

With the flashlight the old man lit the intruder. "Turn around, slowly."

Tristan turned around.

A lot of denim and pockets and a backpack but no obvious weapons.

Facing them again he smiled. "See?"

The light revealed Tristan was missing one front tooth.

"You!" the old man and his daughter said simultaneously.

"Uh, yeah?" Tristan said.

"You followed me," the old man's daughter said.

"I kinda did."

"Even though I told you to take a hike?" She stepped closer, but she uncocked her gun. "And then you come in here without even wearing a mask? What kind of loony are you?"

"I got a mask," Tristan said. "Of course I do." He fished in a pocket, then another. Then he took off his backpack. "OK if I open this?"

"Don't you breathe our air without you wear a mask," the old man said.

The boy couldn't contain himself anymore. "He might have a bomb in there. He might blow us all up. That's how they do it." He lifted his gun and moved toward the stranger.

Almost everyone had backpacks these days but the old man knew that the boy was most upset about what his whole world had become.

His mother moved across to block her son and said, "Well, good luck to us all then."

"Mom!"

"Get the damn mask," the old man said to Tristan and at the same time he took the boy's arm. "It'll be all right."

The boy lowered his gun and Tristan opened his backpack. There was a mask at the top. He put it on.

"Sit on the floor, against the wall," the old man said.

The intruder turned to look for a spot.

"First, close the door."

Tristan closed the door. The old man used the flashlight to show him where to sit.

The family moved their seating boxes to face him. The woman gave her father a disinfectant wipe to clean the flashlight and his hands with.

27

"So why did you come here?" she asked Tristan then.

"I got a house," he said.

"So?"

"A big house. Rooms. Beds."

"So you're one of the richies – goodie for you. But what are you doing *here*?" After a moment, "And at a foodbank?"

"I don't *own* the house," Tristan said. "It's empty. But it's big and I'm there alone."

The family waited. The old man passed the flashlight to his daughter while he put an arm around his grandson's shoulders.

"It's got electricity. Running water. Hot showers. It's even got a yard."

"And you're there alone?" the old man's daughter said.

The old man's auntie's house had more rooms than people, after his mother and Plum died. He remembered hot food more than hot showers. "Got a working stove?" he asked.

"Yeah. And an oven," Tristan said, interrupting what he'd been saying to the woman. "And it'd be so much safer if we was all up there, because if some of *them*…" He held his hands apart.

They all knew about the roving bands that stole from the dispossessed because they were easier prey than stores or richies. The scavengers…

"If some of *them* found me in this empty house there'd be no way I could defend it alone."

Or himself. You're too stupid to live, the old man thought, if you're telling all this to strangers.

"But if we were there together…" Tristan said. "It's win-win, and that's even before I knew you had guns."

"This big house of yours," he said, "it's not in city center, right?"

"Part way up the hill. Not all the way up. Not as far as the checkpoints."

"But anybody sees you – or one of us – walk up that hill carrying stuff, they'd know we were going somewhere. We'd be noticeable – not like if someone sees us walking around here."

"There's gardens where you can lose someone following."

"Hell, I didn't even mange to lose *you*," the woman said.

"Yeah, well, I'm pretty good at following."

"Why her?" the boy said suddenly.

"In the foodbank I saw she had dependents, but nobody was there with her. So I thought maybe we could help each other." He looked lonely and uncomfortable in the light from the flashlight. "When I talked to her she sounded tough. And she looks a bit like my mom did."

"She so ain't *your* mom," the boy said angrily. Then, after a moment, "So who followed *you* here today?"

"Good question," the old man said.

Tristan said, "Well, no one."

"Even with that backpack and all the stuff in your pockets? Walking down into the city from a house part way up the hill?"

"Lots of people carry stuff these days."

"I think you need to go," the woman said.

"Come on," Tristan said, "at least think about it. Big house. Electricity. Hot water. The yard has hedges, no one can see. It's great."

"Enjoy it," the old man said.

"Let me at least tell you where it is, in case you change your mind." He fiddled in his jacket pocket and pulled out a piece of paper. "Directions," he said, putting the paper on the floor. "Maybe feel like a bath. Try it out? Wouldn't you like a nice, hot bath? There's shampoo and everything."

"I'd love a hot bath," the woman said. "Now get the fuck out."

Tristan rose. He approached the door he'd come in through. He stopped and held out a hand.

The old man gave him his flashlight and the unwelcome visitor left, closing the door he hadn't broken down.

The old man was glad to see the intruder go but was more pleased because he felt that his grandson was calmer now. Because he'd spoken out? Or just because the world hadn't come crashing through the door. This time.

The old man and his daughter looked at each other. "Move?" he said.

She nodded. "What are the odds this 'house' really is empty?"

The old man said, "Can't stay here."

"We could have used another flashlight," the boy said.

"We're no scavengers," the old man said.

"Not yet," his daughter said.

"Tell you this, my girl," the old man said. "I don't want you going to the foodbank alone again."

5. PANSY VALIANT

The old man didn't like his grandson going out alone. Nor did his mother but the boy went out by himself every day now, and they had to accept it. Boys would be boys, even in these dangerous times. And at least the old man knew the boy could run fast.

He'd seen it for himself, most dramatically one summer afternoon when his grandson ran down a friend who was on a bicycle and pedaling as hard as he could. The kid had snatched the boy's fudgesicle and, laughing, tried to get away with it. He failed. The boy was nine at the time. The old man had been very impressed.

Back in the day the boy might have been able to do something speed like that. Not be an Olympian or anything, but maybe rate some special attention at school – back when there were schools. Perhaps eventually get a college scholarship.

As a teenager the old man had once been asked to run the 400 yards in a gym class. He set out fast and heard the teacher and other boys cheering him on and sounding surprised at how quickly he was running. For just a moment he'd thought he was good. But after the first 200 yards the cheering stopped. His legs had never felt so heavy and *painful* since.

But the boy was fast. And he was getting stronger too, exercising in doorways by pushing against both jambs simultaneously, using the resistance. The old man had taught him that. You could do it even when you were holed up in a dark, empty store.

The old man's reveries were interrupted when the boy returned from his outing.

"Are you all right?" his mother asked as soon as he was out of his mask. "You've been away a long time."

And he had, the old man thought. Longer than usual.

"Fine, Ma." He looked at her. "I'm *fine*."

"Did anybody stop you?"

"Nobody. No problems, honestly," the boy said, sounding a little impatient. "I've got something I want to tell you."

"Go on," the old man said.

"I've found us a new place to live!"

*

If darkness was one of the requirements of a safe residence, the abandoned store the boy led them to certainly qualified. There was only one window in the ground floor room farthest from the street entrance.

But it didn't smell musty and the old man and his daughter agreed that they could probably make it work. Not least because they needed to move, urgently.

34

And the boy was excited by a find inside. "Look," he said, "Yarn!"

Their flashlights revealed shelves of skeins of yarn in a deep closet. How a yarn store had survived commercially in a narrow side-street in a rundown part of the city didn't concern them now. The boy had a different question. "Why didn't nobody take it?" he asked, holding yarn in each hand.

"Because you can't eat it?" the old man said.

"No needles," his daughter said, peering into the closet, then turning. "I used to knit, you know. But it takes needles."

Is that why they call them *needles*? the old man was thinking as the boy said, "Really?"

"For a while." She addressed her father. "Remember?"

"Her mom taught her the knitting," he said. "Scarves as Christmas presents."

"I never finished a scarf. It was potholders. Thick wool. They kept you from burning your hands."

"And I never once burned a hand while using mine," the old man said with a laugh. Which they both knew meant that he'd never "used" the potholder at all, not least because he didn't do any of the cooking then.

But he did keep the gift on a shelf where he kept souvenirs from his child and his family. A shelf he called his "museum." Back when they had a place of their own; when he had a place he could keep sentimentals.

"Is there a way out at the rear?" the boy's mother asked.

"Yup," the boy said, excitement growing. "And you'll never guess what I found out there. Come on, take a look." He led them through into a small service yard.

Was *this* what was exciting him? the old man wondered. But his grandson carried on to a garage with a dirt encrusted door.

"A car?" his daughter asked.

"Better than that," the boy said. He crouched down and opened the door carefully. He was immediately knocked over by a large brown dog.

The old man ran forward to protect his grandson but the dog was licking the boy's face. "There, there," the boy said. "Good girl. Good girl." He turned to his mother and grandfather with a beaming smile. "Great, isn't she? I'm gonna call her Pansy Valiant. Because she's brave and beautiful. And she can protect us. Be our lookout, so's we can sleep better. Y'know?"

The old man and his daughter looked at each other. It had been a long time since either of them had thought about either bravery or beauty.

"She's got a collar," the boy's mother said as she approached the dog and cautiously extended a hand to be smelled.

"It doesn't say her name. Just a phone number. But she followed me. *Me.*"

*

"So what do you think?" the old man asked as he and his daughter left the former yarn store to walk to the foodbank. There was hardly anyone around. It *was* an out-of-the-way place. Maybe the boy had chosen well.

"I think I'll ask for blankets, if they have them," she said. "It'll be cold soon."

The old man was silent. That's not what he meant. He was sure she knew that.

The foodbank had a schedule for its users. They'd left the boy to continue exploring in the boarded up store.

"We should have made sure the water is still connected," the old man's daughter said eventually.

"Do it when we get back," he said.

"When's the last time we had a place with a backyard, Pa? You going to cut the grass, or do we leave that to him?"

He'd had to cut the grass a lot at his auntie's house, with an old hand mower. He'd worked hard at it and done a good job. She'd always complimented him on the work, the way he cleaned up the cuttings, the way he edged near the sidewalk. But he wasn't cutting the grass for his auntie. It was for her boyfriend. If he did it, then Charlie wouldn't get nagged to do it. And if Charlie was pleased he wouldn't complain so much about three being a crowd.

But there was no grass behind the yarn store. The yard was stones, peppered only by weeds. "That's not what I meant, which you know."

37

"Yeah, Pa."

"There's no way he found the place and came straight back to tell us. He found the dog first."

"I agree."

"Made friends with it. Found *it* a place to stay – maybe that garage. Or maybe the dog led him there. Abandoned by its previous owners? Did you see the water bowl?"

"So we probably won't have to worry about water," she said. "And the food bowl? You saw that too?"

"He's been taking food to it. That's why he's been out on his own a lot recently. And even though we only had cold beans for *our* supper."

"But did you see the light in his eyes, Pa?" the old man's daughter said. "He's crazy about that dog."

"Trying to take care of a dog? Trying to feed it? In times like this? That's *crazy*."

"Yeah, well. Maybe."

"I never had a dog at his age."

"At any age?"

"Well, no," with a little laugh.

"You know how we worry when he goes out alone. It's a big dog."

"But he'll have to go where he can find steak bones and crap a dog would eat even though we wouldn't. Steak bones will only be near richies' houses. How can going up there do anything but put him in more danger?

Scavengers prowl areas like that like wasps on a peach tree. It's a fucking *jungle*."

"I know what it is out there, Pa," she said quietly. "It can be bad enough even downtown."

A lone man was approaching them. He wasn't wearing a mask. They crossed the street and were silent until the guy was behind them and continuing on his way. There were more people on the sidewalks as they neared the foodbank, and a few vehicles on the streets.

"He's smart," the woman said eventually. "He knows how to look after himself. And he did find us our new home."

"Yes."

"I think it'll do for a while."

The old man considered. They'd only examined the empty yarn store quickly because of the foodbank appointment. But it had a big enough room behind the one that bordered its street. There were also stairs to a room above. "Yeah," he said, "once we confirm that there's running water."

"He needs *something*, Pa." She stopped and took his elbow to get him to look at her directly. "Think about the life he's leading."

"Still being alive, you mean?"

"Something of his own. He's fourteen. What's he got of his own?"

"What have any of us got?"

"*We* have our memories, Pa, you and I." She turned. "C'mon. We can't be late."

They walked on in silence. It was a fair point. The boy didn't have much of a previous life to look back on. Sure, a childhood, some friends back in the day. And the boy would remember his grandmother – before she got sick. She'd loved her grandson. She'd baked for him. What's your favorite pie today? she'd ask. And she'd make it if she could. Pumpkin. Pecan. Cherry. She made good pies.

"Do they ever have pies at the bank?" he asked his daughter.

She gripped his arm and pulled him closer. "You're thinking of Ma."

He gave her a squeeze to acknowledge that.

"You know they may not let you come in with me."

"Depends how many are already in there. I know."

"Apart from pies, is there anything special you want me to look for? To ask for?"

"Yeah."

She waited.

"Dogfood," he said.

6. WALK THE WALK

It was the old man's turn to walk with Pansy Valiant. He held a thick cord of braided yarn attached to her collar – a "leash" that was multi-colored, because his grandson thought that was funny.

But it was also plenty strong enough to restrain the dog if she decided to run away – to chase something, say – so why not? Though there were fewer wild things in the city to chase, perhaps most having been killed for food.

However Pansy Valiant seemed sweet-tempered and biddable so far, which was a great relief to them all. Nevertheless the leash was essential. Uncontrolled dogs were shot on sight if they were unlucky enough to be spotted by the remnants of law enforcement.

There weren't many of these uniformed killers in evidence but whenever the old man or his family saw one they scooted the other way. No one trusted uniforms anymore.

"I never had a dog when I was a kid, y'know," the old man said. He'd told this to the others before but Pansy Valiant looked up at him and her expression seemed to say, Tell me more. "Nope, no pets at all. Not even a cockaroach for company." But would a dog be interested in cockaroaches?

"Mom had a hard enough time feeding her and me and Plum while she was alive. Auntie never seemed to be short of money but she wouldn't have seen the point of a dog." He thought about living with his aunt, who did occasionally show him a bit of affection. "Maybe I was her pet."

They walked on along an alley. They were heading west from the new place. The other two had headed east. Next time they'd split up north and south. They needed to know what was in the neighborhood. That was a matter of security and, maybe, opportunity.

"Nope, no pet," the old man said thoughfully. One of his teachers in grade school had kept a caged canary in the classroom for a while but the bird wasn't much company – it didn't sing, or even chirp. Then one Monday Chee-Chee the canary wasn't there. Nor was the cage.

Randy, the class rebel, had asked, "Where's Chee-Chee, Miss?" Without meeting Randy's eyes she'd told the class that she'd decided to keep Chee-Chee at home.

Everyone else giggled because they knew the bird was dead. But that exchange was also the first time the old man realized Chee-Chee was male. He'd always thought of her as a girl canary.

"Why did I think that?" he asked Pansy Valiant. "Because only girls lived in cages?"

Everyone was in cages now.

"I'm supposed to be checking the neighborhood," the old man said then. "Even keeping an eye out for a better place to live." The dog wagged her tail.

"We won't want to stay here forever, Pa," his daughter had said of the former yarn store. And of course he knew that. It was great as a refuge but not as a home. No heat, with winter coming? Yet what would ever count as a "home" these days? And what would count as "forever"?

So they were all out looking for... What? "Hell, Pansy," the old man said, "I don't know what I'm looking *for*."

She turned her friendly eyes toward him again, and again he felt encouraged.

"Do you prefer being called Pansy, or would you like Valiant better? Or maybe Ms Valiant?" He liked the idea of Ms Valiant. It showed respect.

"Ms Valiant," he tried experimentally.

This time the dog sat down and looked up at him. He bent down and scratched behind her ears and she clearly liked it. He stopped scratching and she got up immediately. They walked on together.

His grandson's accidental meeting with this sweet creature was giving him pleasure. But it also scared him. If they lost her...

There'd been too fucking much loss already.

"Maybe I'll find a car," he said, trying to think of something else. "That would give us options."

Well, a car full of gas, or diesel, or an electric charge might. They could get out of "here".

But to go where? He didn't have a clear idea where they might go that was within a tankful's journey. And anyway was life outside the city any easier?

In the country, say, there *were* barns. Straw could be made into comfortable sleeping places. And might they find some surviving chickens? Maybe have eggs, if they contrived a way to cook them? And if they got some seeds, they could grow things.

His grandmother had grown things.

Oh, the *corn* Grandma had grown. And the mangoes. Though what she'd called mangoes the world now called "green peppers." He salivated at the memory of the meals Grandma had made. But she'd died even before his mother and Plum.

And how could they survive somewhere new long enough to be able to *grow* things? However independent he and his daughter and her son might be, the truth was that these days they needed to be close to a foodbank.

The bank was their only reliable source of food and, occasionally, other things. You could only go once every four days, whether they had anything much to give out or not. But that's just how it was, and good luck to you.

So maybe a town rather than out in the country. Somewhere with a yard big enough to grow things.

And maybe because a town was smaller than a city there'd still be some community spirit, with better-off people helping those who weren't. It used to be like that. He and his wife had given money and even time, now and then, to help other people. Were there richies willing to help the poories these days? Somewhere?

He laughed. "In my dreams," he told Pansy Valiant.

And he did sometimes dream of meals, vast tablefuls of food, like a Medieval banquet. Or a Sizzler, like he'd been to once when Auntie was celebrating Charlie's birthday on an all-you-can-eat shrimp day. Ooo, coming back for seconds, and *thirds*...

The old man and Pansy Valiant came to a garage with a closed door – all the others they'd passed were open, empty, looted. Not, surely, a car...

Cautiously, the old man made his way to the side. He found a window frame, one pane knocked out. He looked in.

Instantly a bearded face appeared in front of him, all but nose-to-nose. Unlike his own face, this one wasn't masked. "What do you want?" the man asked fiercely. "Whatchoo lookin' at?"

The old man caught a whiff of recently extinguished candle. He jumped back. "Nothin'," he said. "Nothin'. Just looking around."

"Look around somewhere else!" A batten, sharpened to a point at one end, appeared by the bearded face. "Go on, get out. Get away."

The old man lifted his free hand to show he had no harmful intent and he backed off. Pansy Valiant made a whiny sound. It was the first sound the dog had made the whole walk.

When they were back in the alley the old man stopped and crouched. He put an arm around her. "There there, girl," he said. "It's all right." But she was shaking. Did her reaction to a loud, angry voice tell the old man something about her earlier history?

They carried on. Maybe not a car, the old man thought. How about a bike? Bikes don't need gas.

He thought about what he'd seen on the streets the last few months. A few vehicles – mostly pick-ups – but he couldn't remember a single bike. Did that mean there were hundreds of bikes hidden in richies' sheds up the hill? Or had everyone with a bike already ridden it somewhere "else"? To the make-believe place where things were like they used to be? Back in the day...

He'd first learned to ride on a girls' bike with training wheels. His mom had a friend two doors down. And Gloria let him ride the bike up and down the sidewalk when her own child, Lucy, was playing in the sandbox.

He got so he could ride really fast. And he learned to ride without the training wheels. But then Gloria wouldn't let him on the bike anymore. Lucy had started having tantrums about his using it.

He could have made friends with Lucy, enough that she might want to share, but not long after that the cops had broken down the door and taken his mother away. And then the social workers had taken *him* away.

Later, in high school, he knew a guy whose father had *built* him a bike – out of spare pieces of other bikes. How cool was that!

Maybe he and Pansy Valiant would come across a pile of parts, like a bicycle graveyard. Then they could make themselves bikes, maybe even some to sell. They could really use some *money*. Between them they had almost none. *That* would be something to take back to his daughter and the boy.

"So," he said to the dog, "how smart are you, Ms Valiant? Could you learn to ride a bike?" A little laugh but then a gust of wind reminded him to look at the sky. There was always a haze but clouds were rolling in. "I think we head back now."

He led his companion to the end of a block and they turned down another alley toward "home".

The old man was silent for a long time and Pansy Valiant walked beside him, seeming content with his company.

A car, he thought. If we're going to find a car, how about a nice *old* car. No point in a Cadillac, though, even one with fins – you could only go twenty miles on a tank of gas in one of those. But… Well, he didn't know the names, but how about one of real old-fashioned ones, a roadster like they'd had in black and white movies, back in the day when there were movies.

Yeah, a car with running boards, and a canvas top you could put up or down with the weather. He looked up. It started to sprinkle. Had they turned around too late?

He wondered if the others had kept track of the weather and had gotten home before any rain. If it was heavy it would be hard to dry off.

He crouched again by Pansy Valiant. "Yeah," he said. "Let's have a roadster. Red with black trim and brass fittings. Some fancy I-talian name like Lamborelli. Something that can really move, like we're going to have to."

The dog looked up at him. She whimpered again. "But let me tell you this, Ms Pansy Valiant. If there's no room for you in our roadster, we just won't take it, no matter how much gas it's got."

7. BACK IN THE DAY

The old man waited outside the foodbank while his daughter went in with their list. Although a list was almost a joke. Asking for what you wanted was one thing, but you were only given what the bank happened to have in stock.

Supposedly organized by what was left of state and federal governments, the only official thing supplicants could count on was identification technology that kept track of who they were and what they were given. And when the power was down, people who came to the bank for their scheduled visits were turned away and told to come back later, no matter how desperate they were.

Facemasks were required of course. If you forgot yours, tough. It was a foodbank but there wasn't much charity about the way it operated.

Ironic, the old man thought, because it was housed in an old church. Back in the day everyone was welcome in churches. While banks were about the worship of money, though people like him and his family never saw much of *that*.

Back in the day: his daughter and her son teased him for using that phrase, but how else should he identify the past? "Before there were no more jobs?" "Before banks ran out of money?" "Before we stopped having safe places to live?" Or… "a lifetime ago?"

Once a church had figured big-time for him a lifetime ago. Though he was not a believer in god he was a believer in meeting girls and he'd met his wife at a "social" in one of those churches, back in the day. She was no more a believer than he was but in a world where people didn't ask, "Do you go to church?" only, "What church do you go to?" where else were you supposed to meet girls?

Or boys?

They hit it off immediately. Kept hitting it off for decades.

He missed her so much.

"Hel-lo, Meester sir."

He turned to the voice and found a thin man of perhaps forty – though it was hard to tell when people wore masks and hats. However the man talked with an accent.

"Hello?" the old man said, cautious. People didn't talk to strangers nowadays. And, truth was, few people stood *outside* the bank other than in the lines waiting for their turn.

"You waiting, yes?"

Obviously. "Yes."

"Me not so much," the man said. "Nobody inside getting a foodbox or clothes or nothing for me."

The old man was puzzled. "So what are you doing here?"

"I not allowed."

"No ID card?"

"I lose – it was mugging. Somebody saying it is me now has ID. They see it being used. They won't replace. I can go starve to death." The thin man said it lightly, as if it was a joke.

"That's rough," the old man said.

"Rough, yes," the thin man said. "Yes, very rough."

Though the guy's predicament was sad, it was not that unfamiliar. It seemed like they – "they" – refused help whenever they could. Like, his daughter usually did better in the bank than he would because "they" sometimes wouldn't believe he had two dependents at his age. In any case welfare was a crapshoot. She could come out with an armful or nearly empty.

A crapshoot, he thought. Beginning to remember when he'd seen men – and boys, sometimes only boys – gamble surprisingly large amounts on rolls of dice.

"I from Slovenia," the thin man said.

"What's that?"

"Beautiful famous country."

Not *that* famous, the old man thought.

"We have world-beating bi-cycle racers. But I am not race. I have no bi-cycle. One time, but was stolen."

"It's hard to hang onto anything these days," the old man said.

"Truth," the thin man said, nodding.

They stood studying each other behind their masks.

A woman passed them in a hurry. She was rushing to get into the bank before it closed.

"I am sad," the thin man said, "because no food."

The old man couldn't say much to that, wondering if this stranger expected a handout. But wouldn't he be standing outside a store, up the hill and closer to where the richies shopped? The guy couldn't be thinking the old man had food to spare. Not outside a foodbank. Though he *was* wearing the nearly new tracksuit top his daughter brought home last time. He straightened the top and pulled down its sleeves.

"I carry everything," the thin man said. "Or hide in bushes, under boxes, whatever."

Well, that's the world we live in, the old man thought. Everyone carries their lives on their backs like campers used to, back when camping was optional. Yes, back in the day...

His hip hurt now. Why was there never an easy place to sit anymore? "Yeah," he said at last. "If you can't carry it, you can't keep it."

"Carry or hide," the thin man said. "But I thank you."

What the hell for? the old man thought. Then he said, "What for?"

"You talk to me. Not ignore or spit. You need all your beans and whatever, I know. But you talk."

"And I wish you luck," the old man said, feeling sympathy at last.

"You good man, I see." The thin man looked around, as if to make sure no one was listening. "So I tell you this – I got beer. You want some beer?"

"*What?*"

"My stash, my belongings, I got beer. I find a box. Not far. Would you like? I share. Much better to drink when not alone."

Beer... How long had it been since he tasted *beer*? The old man licked his lips. And then remembered a time being in a car with his grandfather. He was only five but Pop-pop was showing off the little town he hadn't yet been forced to leave. They'd driven past a bar and Pop-pop pointed it out. "Good beer in there," he said. "No Mexicans."

Later he'd wondered why he'd been put in a foster home when he had a grandfather. But on that same car journey Pop-pop had run over the corner of the sidewalk when he was making a turn and didn't notice. A clue?

"You got time for a beer?" the thin man asked. He pointed toward scrubland behind the former church. "Near the river."

If he had to live rough, the old man thought, being near running water would be smart. Better take a chance with river water than try to sneak some at a faucet somewhere, or steal bottled. If you were going to steal, why not steal beer? He chuckled.

"You got time?" the thin man said again.

The old man looked at his watch. How long had his daughter been inside?

"Come," the thin man said. "A bottle beer."

"Who's your friend, Pa?"

The old man turned and saw his daughter almost beside him. She carried two brimming plastic bags and had a blanket over one shoulder. It had been a good day.

"Dunno his name," he said, "but he's from some weird country, Sloveen-something." He turned to the thin man.

But the thin man was backing away.

"Jess?" the old man's daughter said. "Jess? Is that you?"

"Fuck," the thin man said. He turned and ran.

The old man didn't understand.

"Some weird country?" his daughter asked. "Are you kidding me?"

The old man reached for one of the plastic bags she was carrying.

"Here. This one's heavier," she said.

"You *know* that guy?"

"I ought to. I was in high school with him."

They began to walk toward their relatively new "home".

"What'd he want?" the old man's daughter asked.

"We were talking. He was saying how hard a time he was having being foreign and having been mugged for his ID card."

"Foreign? He was spinning you a line, Pa. What did he *want*?" She glanced at him. "Not money, surely."

"He never said he wanted anything. But he offered me some beer. Said he had some nearby."

"Oh *Pa*," she said. "And you were falling for *that*?"

The old man looked back toward the scrubland behind the church. "What *could* he want? My ID wouldn't be any use."

"They try to get workers."

"*What*?"

"Who do you think picks the corn and the apples these days? There would have been guys waiting who'd kidnap you and make you work for them, Pa. I had no idea you were so street-stupid. Honestly, don't you know better than to put your hand out when some stranger offers you candy?"

They walked in silence for a while.

"The boy's going to *love* this," the woman said, "after all the warnings we've given *him*."

But the old man wasn't thinking about his grandson's mirth. He was thinking, They wanted me. *Me*! I guess I'm not so much past it after all.

8. BUTTONS

They had to wait until there was a nighttime power cut. Those were frequent but now that the old man and his family *wanted* one… "Does watched power never cut?" the old man's daughter asked.

The old man smiled ruefully. Having prepared a plan involving them all, waiting wasn't easy. Sleeping when you knew you might have to get up quickly made you restless.

"What is it that knocks the power out?" the boy asked as he pulled Pansy Valiant close.

"Maybe when there isn't enough wind?" his mother suggested.

But the boy said, "Aren't the richies still boiling up water to put in their Jacuzzi things? Or baking cakes? Or roasting… whatever they roast at night?" He buried his face in the dog's furry neck.

"I bet most of the richies have generators of their own."

That made the old man wonder if there was a way he could build a generator, even if it was just for some electric light. They got candles from the foodbank but that was hardly the same. There must be metal junk around the city. What would it take to make a small windmill, say…?

But, in fact, they didn't have to wait long for the city's electricity to go down. On the third night, streetlights flickered out at about one a.m.

The old man, who was on watch, roused the others. They quickly dressed in the darkest clothes they had.

*

Their target, a camping supplies store, was about two miles to the north of their current "home". It was in the foothills – not in the city center but also not up the hill – and by taking turns they'd been able to reconnoiter without arousing suspicion.

The old man's daughter was the only one who'd been approached by anyone. A swarthy man had crossed the street to ask what she was doing. "Window shopping," she'd said. "That's the only kind of shopping I can afford these days."

"He wasn't interested after that," she'd reported, brushing her hair back with a hand. "Do you think I've lost my allure now that I have no purchasing power?"

The plan was to break the glass in a bathroom window, then get in and out quickly. The power cut was key because it would eliminate any alarm system along with the streetlights.

As usual, the old man acted as lookout. He and Pansy Valiant stood on the sidewalk. The dog had a new blackout leash plaited from black and dark brown yarns.

The old man held his free hand to an ear. Anyone driving past and noticing him would think he was on the phone, although it had been a very long time since he'd had anything resembling a working phone. Not that he expected many vehicles to be on the street at this time of night. Still, you had to be careful.

Then he did see headlights. Antsy, he stepped into a shadow but the truck didn't even slow down.

The dog whimpered. He knelt by her. "What's the matter, girl?" But he knew. Anxiety was contagious.

He never used to be a thief. Oh, maybe a few things of no consequence. A traffic cone, because it was funny to have outside his room door, until Auntie's boyfriend hit him on the head with it. Flowers for his wife once from in front of a supermarket. A pen or two when he worked where there was stationery. OK – maybe more than a pen. But not breaking and entering like this – for a camp stove and the gas to fuel it. And… And whatever else his daughter could find while she was inside. Anything that would help them now the weather was on the turn.

He didn't feel good about stealing. "But needs must," he told Pansy Valiant. "How else we gonna get by?"

And that was what mattered. He'd promised his wife. With almost her last breath she'd said, "Look after them."

"I will," he promised.

If she said anything else it was lost in the racket of the ventilator. She was one of the last to rate a ventilator, for all the good it did.

But he'd promised, so he *was* trying to look after them. And the task was to focus on the here, the now.

But to be standing on the sidewalk felt feeble in the "taking care of" department when his daughter and her son were doing all the actual work.

Still, they were more agile and quicker than he was. That was just a fact.

He hummed a song, "Stayin' Alive". His grandson wouldn't know it. Would his daughter? "You know that one?" he asked the dog.

He shuffled with a bit of rhythm, but also because it was cold. And it was going to get colder. That was the point.

Then he knelt down and put his arms around the dog to see if she was shivering. Not yet.

"Hey!" The deep voice seemed to have come out of nowhere.

The old man shot up to face a dark mountain of a man in black: dark hat, dark clothes, dark face. There was not enough ambient light to see him properly.

"Hey yourself," the old man said bravely. He pulled Pansy Valiant close. Then held up the leash as if there was light enough from the few stars and the gibbous moon shining through the haze to see it. "Under control," he said.

"I don't give a fuck about that," the man mountain said. "I want to know who you are and what you think you're doing out here at this time in the morning."

"Walking the dog, Sir," the old man said. "I have ID."

The man mountain pulled out a flashlight. It too was huge.

"Do *you* have ID?" the old man asked.

"You shittin' me?" But as the mountain bent forward to see the old man's card, reflected light showed a jacket with gleaming buttons, including two on his shoulders. That proved the mountain's official status. The buttons were made of real gold. Or so the old man had heard.

Buttons Man studied the old man's ID, but didn't touch it. "What's your date of birth?" he asked.

The old man gave it, quickly.

"Security code?"

The old man provided that too.

The Buttons stood straight again and shined the beam on Pansy Valiant, who retreated farther behind the old man's legs. "And you're walking the dog?" He reached around and grabbed her collar.

"Yeah," the old man said. "And she's had all her shots." Then, "C'mon, girl. Do your business so's we can go home." Pansy Valiant stared at him, uncomprehending.

The big man rotated the dog's collar, studying that now. "Phone number," he said.

"Yeah. But no phone no more."

"I hear you," the Buttons said. "Where's your damn mask, old timer?"

"Here, here in my pocket," the old man said, fumbling to pull out his mask, and furious with himself. "I didn't expect to run into anyone this time of night. Sorry. Sorry." He slipped the mask on and adjusted it to fit his face.

"They can carry it, you know."

"Sir?"

"Dogs. It can linger in their fur."

"We wash her regular," the old man said. Then immediately regretted his choice of words.

The Buttons heard. "We?"

"My daughter and me and her son."

"Where are they?"

"My turn to take the dog out." The old man shrugged.

The Buttons paused. "What are you doing outside a camping store?"

"Is that what it is?" The old man looked. "Oh yeah." He turned back. "I went camping once, you know."

Silence.

"Back in the day. My father-in-law and my wife's brother. We rented tents for a weekend, my wife and me, and them. But what I remember best was the net and rackets for badmitten. You know it? Net between poles and you hit this little feathery thing back and forth, a shufflecock. But thing was – and I didn't have a clue – my father-in-law was some kind of demon at

62

badmitten, some kind of big deal player." He shook his head with the memory. Babbling, but it seemed the safest thing to do. When would the Buttons get bored?

"I mean, how was I supposed to guess that? Basketball, baseball, even golf, sure. *Real people* play those games. Maybe somewheres they still do. But *badmitten*? The guy pounded the damn shufflecock down my throat every time I hit it and there wasn't a damn thing I could do about it. I'd hold my paddle on the left and he'd hit it to the right, hold it right and it goes past my left ear. And then sometimes he smacks it straight at me, just to make a change. He thought it was hilarious, and so did my wife's brother. My wife didn't laugh though. She was good like that, always on my side, y'know. I really miss her." He paused for breath.

"What the hell are you telling me about?" the Buttons said. "Why you doing that? You nervous?"

"Course I'm nervous. You got a gun, I bet."

"Yeah. I got a gun. You got a gun?"

"Of course not."

"Let's see, shall we?"

The old man knew what was coming next and was ready for it. He put his arms up and from another pocket the Buttons pulled a scanner that looked like a shoe and he flipped a switch.

But there was no reaction as the shoe passed around the old man's body.

The old man said, "You need me to tell you my dog's name for your records? She's called Whiskers. My wife used to have a cat called that and–"

"I protect property," the huge man said. "Not dogs."

"So you'd protect me? Someone came along to steal my dog?" He patted Pansy Valiant.

The huge gold buttoned man chuckled.

Which made the old man feel a little safer, though he was worried about the time that had passed and whether his daughter and the boy might hurry around the corner of the store, eager to get away and without being careful.

"How long you got to be out here," the old man asked.

"How long *you* out here?"

"Long enough to get fucking cold. Time to go head home now," the old man said. "Walk with me? Keep me safe? I'm going that way." He pointed behind him, in the direction the Buttons had already been heading.

"Yeah, all right I guess. As long as you keep that mask on and your mouth shut. You talking like that will warn people I'm coming."

"What people?"

"People out in the dark, up to no good."

"Got it, got it," the old man said. He pulled Pansy Valiant up from where she sat. "Me quiet, like a tomb."

They walked in silence to the end of the block and the old man began to feel better. Not just because they were out of sight of the store but because he'd done his job. He'd been useful. Contributed.

"So tell me about yourself," he said to the Buttons after they crossed a street. "Where'd you grow up? How'd you get this job? What church do you go to?"

9. HEAT

"Who'd ever have thought a hot meal could be such a blast," the old man said. "Just the fact of it."

"And *hot* coffee," his daughter said.

The family sat around an improvised table eating macaroni cheese from new metal camping plates and using metal camping knives and forks. Only the boy was picking at his food.

"What's wrong?" the old man asked him.

"Listen to yourselves." He didn't look up – just stared at his plate as if it was dirty.

"What do you mean?" The old man glanced at his daughter. "Having hot food at last, after so long without it… That isn't a big deal?"

"Is this *all* you want now?" His grandson gestured to their plates, and then to their stock of cans. "*Hot* pork and beans; *hot* pea soup; *hot* beef and potatoes?" He shook his head. "Hot deal. Isn't there more to life than a pan you can heat?"

The old man didn't understand his grandson's attitude. The raid on the camping store had been carefully planned and the boy had joined in the process with enthusiasm. They'd come away with not only the little stove to cook on but a small heater able to warm any room they were in. And gas canisters for both. The store had been like a gold mine for the boy and his mother – now they even had sleeping bags and groundsheets. Their backpacks had been filled to bursting, and they'd carried plastic bags too – altogether almost more than they could manage.

When they got safely home after the raid the boy had strutted like the cock of the walk. But now, suddenly, it was as if nothing would ever satisfy him again.

The boy took another mouthful. The look on his face suggested he was chewing dry feathers.

"Of course we want to get out of here," his mother said. "But meanwhile—"

"I know. I *know*," the boy interrupted. "I've heard it all before."

His mother dropped the subject but her look, as she turned to her father, was one of disappointment and confusion. The old man shrugged – he's a teenager? – and returned to his food.

When he was a boy the old man had sometimes complained about meals. Like when his aunt's boyfriend would bring home Mexican food, on purpose. Back then he hated Mexican food: it was sloppy, full of beans and so spicy it seemed like it made his gums bleed. Charlie said it would make a "man" out of him. The old man shook his head.

Usually the boy loved their mac and cheese, even stone cold. The old man's wife had made hers hot and cheesy. OK, so canned mac and cheese didn't cut it by comparison but it was still comfort food, as his daughter called it. The damn kid was spoiling any comfort, any sense of celebration.

The old man sipped his coffee.

He never drank coffee before he got married. His wife made him a cup because she loved it and soon he was hooked. Was it *because* she loved her coffee and he wanted to love what she loved? Or just that his tastes had matured and broadened? Nowadays he took it black and without sugar.

As if there was any choice.

"More?" his daughter asked her son eventually, holding up the saucepan.

The boy waved a hand. The old man read this as meaning Yes.

But his daughter repeated, "Would you like more?" She waited before adding, "Talk to me or go hungry."

"Go on," the boy finally said. He pushed his plate a few inches closer to his mother.

It was cutting a deal, and the boy's mother scooped a good second portion onto the plate.

The old man was aware that his daughter didn't draw lines like this often, life being so weird and stressful anyway these days. But he guessed she felt she had to play the heavy from time to time to give her son something to fight against. Something safe. There was never any question of her love for him.

The old man wondered what his wife would have made of the moody teenager her beloved grandson was now?

"None for Pansy Valiant?" the boy asked then, returning to provocativeness after having given in.

"She's got her own," his mother said.

"You don't think she'd like some hot? Not good enough to have hot food? We have a fourth plate and another fork."

"You show me Pansy Valiant using a fork and next time I'll serve her first," his mother said.

The boy tipped his head, half-acknowledging a mistake in having mentioned the fork. But then he took his plate from the table, left the box he was sitting on, and dropped to the floor beside his dog.

Pansy Valiant looked up from her bowl. She wagged her tail as the boy balanced a knob of mac and cheese on his fork and presented it to her. She took it delicately between her teeth, then wolfed it down.

The boy looked up at the adults with a triumphant smirk.

The old man wanted to laugh but he held his hands out toward his daughter, palms down, silently urging her to say nothing critical. Let it go.

But she didn't need his advice. "More for you, Pa?"

"A little, please," the old man said, seeing what was left in the pan. He wanted to make sure there was still plenty for her to fill up on.

A few minutes later his daughter opened a pack of cookies for dessert. She counted out seven: two each plus one for Pansy Valiant, a peace gesture.

The boy accepted them without comment, sarcastic or otherwise.

The old man and his daughter exchanged glances. Peace had been restored.

"You know, the first cookies were nothing more than dried pieces of bread," the old man said. "Sailors had 'em and they'd last forever at sea. It wasn't till, like, a hundred years ago that anybody thought to sweeten them and make them softer so you didn't have to soak them in water, or gravy from your meal."

"How do you know that, Pa?" his daughter asked.

"I don't know. I just do."

And then he remembered how he knew. One of his schools had a library with a series of histories about a variety of American subjects. He'd devoured them once he ran out of science fiction. He read about the Lewis and Clark expedition, the War of 1812, all sorts.

"You know," he said as he dipped his cookie in what remained of his coffee, "the first trans-continental railroad line was built by one construction team coming from the west meeting up with another coming from the east. And the final spike that connected them was made out of gold."

"We should find it and dig it up," the boy said. "How hard can it be? Just follow the tracks. We could sell it and *buy* things – instead of having get charity from foodbanks or steal all the time."

Was *that* what was eating at him? the old man wondered. The charity? The stealing? The damn kid: like he'd heard of a better way for them to survive?

Well, if that was his problem there wasn't much to be done about it. They had to keep alive.

"What time is it?" the boy said suddenly.

That caught the old man by surprise too, but he told his grandson the time.

"I got to take Pansy Valiant for her walk." The boy presented his empty plate for the dog to lick clean. Which didn't take long.

The old man and his daughter watched silently as the youngster rapidly selected a leash. He shrugged into his jacket and took a few seconds to make sure his collar was neat.

"See you later," he said, making for the door.

"Be careful," his mother said.

"Don't forget your mask," the old man said.

The boy patted his pocket, but then stopped and put the mask on. "Come on, girl."

The old man and his daughter watched the boy and the dog leave. They turned to each other and nodded. The old man said it first. "He's met someone."

"Someone who has him thinking about *buying* things?" his daughter said. "Where's *that* gonna lead?"

10. YARN

It was a risk, but the old man and his daughter decided it was worth taking.

However they had a planning obstacle: they needed to go out at a specific time during the day without the boy coming too. What reason could they give if he said, "I feel like a walk. I'll get my jacket." It wasn't a foodbank day: he knew that schedule. And otherwise all any of them did outside their current home, the former yarn store, was explore this part of the city or walk their dog.

Some afternoons the boy was eager to take Pansy Valiant and wander the alleys and smaller streets, looking for anything that might help them. But other times he joined one of the adults, or stayed behind to doodle on the backs of invoices and order forms that they'd found in a desk upstairs. Was he becoming a poet, an artist, a diarist…? The old man didn't know. The boy wouldn't show anyone what he was doing.

If it came to it, the old man and his daughter decided, they would separate. Whoever the boy wasn't with would keep the appointment.

As decision time approached the old man looked for signs of his grandson's mood. But in the event the problem solved itself. The boy went out after lunch with Pansy Valiant as if it was what he'd always had in mind.

Sure the old man and his daughter would have preferred to have the dog with them. Pansy Valiant had turned out to be the gentlest of souls, but she was big: a stranger wouldn't at first see past her size. Maybe one day they could they train her to growl on cue.

Not that it was sensible to plan anything too far ahead these days.

Having their new family member did sometimes strain their supplies. So far, she seemed ready to eat anything – which was just as well. But how long could a dog be fed on pork and beans and stay healthy?

One of their neighborhood discoveries was a general store that was nearby. It might have dogfood. "Why don't we rob it and see, Pa?" the boy's mother had asked when, delighted, she and her son came back with news of a small but apparently well-stocked emporium only four blocks away.

"No," the old man had said.

When he was a schoolboy he'd read a science fiction book about a guy sent alone to another planet where he lived in a cave. Outside the cave entrance animals grazed and didn't seem to notice him. They were wild gazelle-like fantasy creatures.

But the guy did *not* kill and eat any of them, always going farther afield to hunt. Why? Because if he ever got hurt and *couldn't* do distances then these beasts –

wildezelles? – would still be there to provide food when he really needed it.

"We won't rob the store unless we're desperate and have nowhere else to go," the old man said. "It's *too* close."

The others seemed to feel knocked back, after their excitement about having found it. But they did understand that it was there if they needed it. And if anything was a truth in the world they now inhabited, it was that you never knew what trouble was going to appear next.

*

When the boy and dog had gone, the old man prepared to go out with his daughter. But caution ruled. "So you're really sure you believed her?"

"I told you, Pa. She's about a hundred and eighty – like you. I don't think she had it in her to lie."

"But if someone put her up to it?"

"Like she was an agent of some kind? Come on. She was two places ahead of me at the foodbank. I barely heard her. If it was a set-up they would have made it clearer than that. And why would they target me? They couldn't have had any idea what I could get my hands on."

The old man was reassured but you could also never tell what "they" were thinking when things happened. "They" had behaved in such an unpredictable way back when there was still broadcast news about what "they" were up to. Maybe nowadays the Buttons were paid a bounty for every family group they could locate that might be harvested for labor. Or perhaps "they" were paranoid about contraband or stolen goods. Who knew?

"Anyway," his daughter said, "you didn't talk to her and I did. And I think she's straight."

So they would take the chance.

The old man watched while his daughter filled her backpack with yarn.

*

The meet was to take place in what used to be a children's playground. No wood or metal was left from the swings and slides and roundabouts, but you could see where they used to be. When someone got an idea how to benefit from buried cement mountings those would be gone too.

The old man also made out the footprints where benches for the parents and fences to enclose the playspace had been. Now it was all just rough open ground, and not much of it green.

Auntie's house had been across the street from a little playground but the old man rarely tried to play there. It was haunted in all seasons by a group of older boys who entertained themselves by throwing things at younger children – stones, sticks, even fruit from trees planted on the playground's edge. It was no more fun being hit with an over-ripe pear than with an icy snowball.

But today there were no children, young or old, in this playground. No one at all was there. Nevertheless the old man and his daughter arrived early and approached cautiously, moving slowly from one sheltering spot to another.

At last an elderly woman entered from the other side. She did look a hundred and eighty. The old man could see that her face was all but corrugated.

"She doesn't *look* dangerous," the old man whispered. "I'll give you that."

The ancient woman carried a cane, and pulled along what looked like a piece of carry-on luggage.

Back in the day, the old man thought, ordinary people could get onto airplanes to go for *vacations*. His grandson barely believed such things had ever existed.

At least his daughter had been on a trip like that. The family flew once to Chicago. Back in the day. They'd walked around and ridden the L; they'd gone to a museum, and a *movie*. One with singing and dancing, though he didn't remember its name. His wife would have remembered it. She had a sharp memory for details. She could remember the clothes people wore, names of songs. Amazing.

The truth was that the boy hadn't had a real childhood at all. Sure, when he was little he went to school. But schools changed so much that as he got older they were nothing like what the old man remembered. Or what his daughter remembered. Well before the boy approached his teens, teaching had been abandoned altogether – at least for those who lived in the city and couldn't pay private tutors. He'd never played ball or gone to a friend's house. He'd missed out on so much for so long.

Now *maybe* he'd met someone, but how could *that* have happened?

The old man shook himself, realizing that his daughter was in the middle of nowhere talking mask-to-mask with a woman who looked like his grandma's granny. But he wasn't supposed to be looking at them. He was supposed to be looking everywhere else. Had anyone followed the granny? Was anyone there to rob his daughter of her yarn? Or take her captive. Or… His hand was in a pocket fingering his gun.

But he saw no one. The only other living things nearby were trees from which lower branches had been ripped for firewood.

*

On the way back the old man asked that they stop for a moment.

"You out of breath again, Pa?"

"No no. I'm fine. I just want to…" He tilted his head.

"Ah," his daughter said. They edged into a former doorway, having looked up and down the sidewalk and seen no pedestrians.

Cautiously she showed him.

"I'll be damned," he said. "Money."

"I'd almost forgotten what it looks like."

"What did she say about why she had it?"

"Kept some under her mattress."

"At least she has a mattress," he said.

"And now she has enough yarn to knit… whatever."

"For the winter?"

"Enough for the rest of her life is what she said. Might be the same thing, at her age."

"And you were right about her," the old man said.

"As long as no one *is* following us."

They were extra cautious about returning to their neighborhood, their route circuitous. Then they separated.

The old man headed back to the yarn store, their cave. He expected to find the boy and the dog. "I won't be long, Pa," his daughter said.

*

As the old man arrived, the boy was holding up a rusty piece of metal.

"Whatcha got?" the old man asked.

"Thought we could make it into a spear."

The old man looked around for the dog. Surely nothing had… But yes, there she was, lying quietly on the boy's sleeping bag.

"A spear, eh?" The old man examined the metal pole. It was hollow and rusted at one end. "If we file the rusty end away somehow, it'd make… more a dagger. But it's a good find, boy."

"It was quiet out there. Pretty boring."

"I like to hear about boring. I hope you didn't let your guard down."

"No problems, Grandpa." The boy looked around, "Where's Mom?"

"She'll be back soon."

A frown creased the boy's face. "What's she doin'?"

Instead of continuing the conversation, the old man went to the stack of booty from the camping store. He got out the little stove and a can of gas.

The boy's face lit up. "Early?" The boy looked toward their stock of cans. "Can we have spaghetti and meatballs?"

Pansy Valiant walked over to see what was happening.

"We'll see what your mom says, but you got my vote."

Then the old man's daughter walked in.

"We're cooking an early dinner, Mom," the boy said.

"Yup," his mother said.

"You knew?"

"Pa and I talked about it."

"Can we have spaghetti and meatballs?"

"Why not." She smiled teasingly. "And look what else I've got." From her backpack she pulled four cans of dogfood.

The boy's mouth fell open. He looked at Pansy Valiant with a big smile. The dog looked back, knowing she was receiving attention.

"Where'd you get that, Mom?"

"From the store up the street."

The boy blinked.

"I bought it."

"*Bought* it? How?"

"Money."

"But I didn't know you *had* any," the boy said.

"Just a little. For special occasions."

"Do you hear that, Pansy Valiant?" the boy said, hugging the appreciative dog. "You're a special occasion."

The old man smiled.

"And look what else I've got." His daughter carefully withdrew a small white box from a side pocket.

"What?" the boy said, looking up.

She opened it and pulled out an iced cupcake. "Happy birthday, son."

The boy couldn't believe it.

"I'm afraid it won't take fifteen of our candles, but at least you have the cake."

"Oh Mom!"

"You've missed out on so much that I wish I could give you, but here." She held the cupcake out. "Chocolate all right?"

"Wonderful," the boy said. He rushed to her. "You're the best mom in the world."

The old man felt tears in his eyes, remembering times when his daughter had told *her* mother exactly the same thing.

11. TRADE-OFF

When the birthday boy went out with Pansy Valiant in the early evening the old man was pleased to have the chance to speak alone with his daughter. "You were later getting back from the store than I expected. Was there a problem?" He turned to her from the sink where he was washing up the dinner dishes as best he could by candlelight.

"Yes and no," she said, folding clothes that had dried after being hung up in the family's main room. So many things were nicer in the old yarn store now that they had a little heat.

"Was it with the storekeeper?"

"He *was* a surprise, Pa. A chubby little guy who obviously smokes."

"I didn't think there were any smokers left."

"He reeked of the stuff."

They paused and briefly the old man turned back to the dishes. Perhaps his daughter too was thinking about the scam when a fake scientist announced that smoking sixty-a-day protected lungs from the sickness.

Tobacco sales briefly went through the roof. Had the "scientist" been hired and publicized by a tobacco company? It was a court case that would never come to trial now. But the spike in deaths that followed the fake news had been real enough.

The old man sighed. Knowledge about the sickness and what treatments were effective must have accumulated year by year. But there was no longer any way to get news – fake or otherwise – to ordinary people. Posters occasionally appeared on walls, and by the entrance of the foodbank, but who knew what to trust?

When he was finished, the old man sat on the floor facing his daughter. "So, your experience spending *money* at a store? Did you remember how?" A little chuckle.

"The mask didn't protect me from the smoker-stench," she said. "But as he took my temperature he said he hadn't seen me in his store before. And that I was very welcome."

"What did you say to that?"

"I said I'd been saving what little money I have for my son's birthday and that my son has a dog."

"And?"

"He seemed surprised by both statements, but I *was* buying a cupcake and dogfood. Y'know what, Pa? I think he thought I was a hooker."

"*No...*" the old man said.

"Maybe it's only city hookers who have dogs and ready cash."

Although his daughter's tone was light, the old man was offended. His daughter – his only child – had been insulted by a fat smoker. He hated the man, sight unseen. He glanced to the corner where they kept their guns. Maybe they *should* rob his store, to pay him back for the insult.

"Everything else was fine. He kept his distance and disinfected the change he gave me. I didn't mean to worry you, Pa. But the store owner wasn't what slowed me down."

"No?"

"When I left, a guy in an alley across the way came over to talk to me."

What *now*? "What guy? What *kind* of guy?"

"He did not take me for a hooker." But she laughed and, tossed her hair. "How *you* doin', good lookin'?"

"Stop it," the old man said. His daughter was small and although she was strong she'd be no match for a big man. He should never have left her out there on her own.

But the store was nearby and they'd agreed he should come back to check on the boy. Sometimes the old man felt torn in two. Even if all three of them went everywhere together, there were no guarantees. At least he should've insisted that she take the gun.

But his daughter was describing her conversation with the stranger who'd approached her in the street.

"'…seen you here before.' And I said, 'What's it to you?' And he said, 'Nothin', nothin', it's just maybe I can help you out sometime.'"

"Help you?" the old man said. He wasn't quite up with her story and was breathing heavily despite himself.

"He asked if I'd been buying things in the store – which I obviously had."

"And?"

"And he asked what I'd bought and what I'd paid."

"What kind of thing is *that* to ask a stranger?" It seemed intrusive and personal. "I hope he at least kept his distance."

"He had a mask, Pa," she said, seemingly unconcerned. "And he was keeping well away. So I told him what I'd bought and he shook his head and said, 'You don't look that gullible.'" She laughed. "Gullible and a hooker in one day. How lucky can a woman get?"

But she must have noticed her father's outrage because she went on quickly, "He said he might not be able to get the exact cupcake next time, but dogfood would be easy. Just let him know what I wanted and when. I asked how much and he made it two-thirds what I'd just paid, though I'm sure I could beat him down further."

"A black-marketeer," the old man said, finally understanding. He took a deep breath. He felt relieved. "Hanging around outside a store?"

His daughter nodded.

"And across the street, so the storekeeper wouldn't call his pals or even a Buttons to keep somebody from undercutting him."

"It felt like Facebook used to be, Pa. You'd buy something online and all of a sudden you'd get ads for what you just bought and didn't need anymore."

The old man had never known much about Facebook but he got the idea as his daughter sighed, maybe thinking about a time when buying things, even useless things, was an easy daily event. "Good" old days?

"So what did you do?" he asked.

"I went back to his alley with him and asked what else he could get if I had the money."

"*Do* you have money left?"

"Not much. But as a potential customer he wasn't going to rob me or hurt me, was he? And I wasn't scared of him, Pa. I really wasn't."

"So what *can* he get?"

"He claims he can supply all kinds of food, and a lot of hardware supplies – like fuel for our cooker and heater. He can get winter clothes and blankets. And…"

"And?"

"If I want something unusual or specific, he says he can probably get it if I give him some time."

"Not just a black-marketeer," the old man said. "A fence who can commission stealing to order." He tried to get his head around his daughter's experience.

"He's our first contact with someone who deals in stolen goods, Pa."

"Except for ourselves, of course."

She tilted her head, acknowledging that they were, indeed, thieves. "I figured people like him had to be out there. I just hadn't met one before."

"Because we've never gone to stores as customers before."

The old man sighed heavily, aware again that he hadn't managed to bring any money when he and his daughter and the boy had to leave their real home. Their bank had collapsed before he got to it.

But even if he had managed to pocket his savings would he have lost it all to the sharpsters who were offering vaccines under the counter for a huge price? Back in the day when the uninformed, like himself, still believed there *was* a vaccine that remained effective for longer than it took the sickness to mutate.

Maybe there *was* a broad spectrum vaccine now. Only the richies would know for sure. He and his family would never be told.

"Pa?"

"Sorry." He tried to clear his head. "It sounds like you trusted this guy."

"Only as long as we have a mutual interest. But before I left him I asked for a way to get in touch if there was something I wanted."

"And?"

"I've got a location where I can leave a message if I don't find him in his alley."

"But isn't it a matter of your having some money?"

"Pa…?"

"Yeah?"

"Think about it. If this guy is selling, he also has to be ready to buy."

"You mean if we steal stuff that we don't want for ourselves?"

"Exactly."

The old man frowned. Stealing to survive was one thing but… "Why would we do *that*?"

"*For* the money, Pa. There are things money can buy that we *can't* steal."

"O-K… So, did you keep a way to contact the woman we sold some of our yarn to this afternoon? In case she wants more, or turns out to be the Big Needle for an underground knitting circle?"

"As a matter of fact, I did."

He gave a short laugh. "I suppose we do need to maintain all the contacts we might be able to use."

"But there's more to it than that, Pa."

"What do you mean?"

"Think about it. This guy today was hanging around a tiny store down here in the city. He's small-time. But if he can get almost anything he must have connections higher up the hill."

The old man was confused again. "What might we want from up the hill?"

"Someone who can get us out of here," she said patiently. "This guy might know a guy who knows a guy…"

At last he got it. "Who might be able to get us to somewhere safe…"

"Somewhere we can sustain ourselves without risk."

"If there is such a place."

They stared at each other – neither quite ready to admit to hoping out loud.

12. RISK

"So where the hell is he?" the old man asked his daughter. He checked his watch again. "He's always home by now."

"I don't know, Pa," his daughter said, stating the obvious from across the room. She was on her knees pushing yarn into cracks in the wall to prevent drafts getting in and light getting out.

The old man was doing the same on the opposite wall, but higher up. He needed to leave the knee-work to younger joints.

"He's gone out five days at the same time. What does a fifteen-year-old do in this day and age that depends on the sun going down? Is he a vampire?" Then, "Sorry, that's just stupid. But I'm..." What was he? "I'm worried. I'm afraid."

His daughter stood and came over to him. "We've talked till we're blue in the face about his keeping safe."

"But has he taken any of it *in*? Do children ever listen? Did you?"

"I'll take the Fifth on that, Pa."

The old man sighed and dropped the skein of yarn he'd been working with. "Fuck this. I need a coffee."

"Or a sedative?"

"What I *really* need is to go out looking for him."

"And just where would you go, Pa?"

He shook his head. Of course he had no idea where he'd go. "Maybe follow him tomorrow when he goes out?"

His daughter got out the camping stove and handed him a pan to fill with water.

"I'm not just being paranoid," he said.

"It's worrying, I agree."

A few minutes later they each held a metal cup of hot black coffee.

The old man said, "Maybe he's found a gang of other fifteen-year-olds who throw rocks at Buttons and run away. Or..."

"Who read the Bible to each other?"

"Every kid in the city *has* to be going crazy – parents telling them don't do this, it's not safe to do that."

"If they still have parents," she said.

He blew across his drink and sipped. "I know I'm grasping at straws here." Then, "Remember when there were straws?"

"But you're right – kids everywhere must be wishing for some kind of bigger life."

He looked at her. "Could he have found a bunch from up the hill? Smug teenage richies who come down to try to find poories to slum it with?" He shook his head. "I hope they wear masks."

"He doesn't seem much changed when he's here."

"I disagree. He spends more time than ever upstairs – drawing or writing or whatever it is he does."

"I agree that something's up, Pa. And we don't know what."

The old man sighed. "I'm so very grateful to have you, love. And your troublesome son. You were a handful too, in your day. Is that where he gets it from?"

"Blame the woman, right?"

"Works for me."

They sat in silence for a bit.

Then he said, "He wouldn't be going on the rob by himself, would he?"

"That's not likely."

The old man hadn't seen the boy bring any "things" into their current home. But who knew? "Should we look upstairs?"

"I don't want to invade his space, Pa. It's all he's got to call his own."

"Apart from Pansy Valiant."

"That dog's been a godsend for him."

"And for us. Except that she has to be walked…"

"At the same time every evening, it would seem. Maybe they meet another dog so Pansy Valiant can have a play-date. You want more water in that?"

The old man shook his head. "You haven't seen notices about bounties being paid for anything, have you?"

"Bounties?"

"For rats, or snakes?" He tried to visualize the noticeboard outside the foodbank but he hadn't been there for a while.

"Do you really think there's enough government left to care about rats down here? Up the hill, maybe."

"Or snakes...?" the old man said. "I heard that somewhere they paid for dead snakes. But after a while people started to breed them so they could kill them for the bounty."

"You have my son breeding snakes now?" The old man's daughter laughed.

"I'm worried about him, all right? He's my only grandson." Immediately he regretted using the word "only".

"I'm perfectly aware of that fact," his daughter said stiffly. She rose, emptied her cup in the sink, and went back to where she'd been working on the wall.

The old man sat where he was, feeling bad.

When his daughter was about the same age as the boy was now she'd been raped. And it resulted in a pregnancy. "Bad luck," their doctor called it. Like the rape wasn't bad luck enough.

Although he and his wife would have helped raise the child if she'd wanted to keep it, she didn't and seemed appalled by the very idea.

The old man would have killed the guy if he had ever caught up with him. But his daughter said she didn't know who it was and wouldn't help him try to find out.

"Leave it," his wife told him. "In this, it isn't your place to interfere. It's women's work. She knows best what she needs."

So he'd left it. But even now the old man sometimes thought about the child who might have been his older granddaughter or grandson.

Years later their daughter found the boy's father and had a happy decade with him. But he died in the second wave.

Her mother died in the fourth wave. His wife. His beloved wife who he missed every day.

But it was his responsibility now to look after what was left of his family. And he had to do it without the woman who'd looked after him.

Which was what he was doing in the tiniest way by filling cracks with yarn.

Which was what he was doing by worrying about his overdue grandson.

"I only meant how much I care about him. And his mother. I worry about him. Both of you." The old man looked at his watch again. "Where the *hell* can he be?"

"Arranging a surprise party for us, Pa? Remember to act surprised."

They worked on in silence.

And then suddenly they heard noises outside the old yarn store. Voices.

Leaving their respective walls they both faced the door, straining to hear. The old man wondered if he should get out one of their guns.

But the door opened and Pansy Valiant bounded in, tail wagging, greeting first the old man and then his daughter.

A moment later the boy appeared in the doorway.

He was alive! He didn't look damaged!

But he was frowning. "Mom? Grandpa?"

"What?" both adults said simultaneously.

"Don't be mad."

"About what?" the old man said. His daughter took a step toward her son.

"I…" he began, but then he turned and gestured.

A skinny, scruffy girl came to stand behind him.

"This… this is Mandy. She's my friend and she needs a place to stay real bad. I said she can stay here." The boy paused. "OK?"

13. CHARM

The old man was out with his grandson, just the two of them. That didn't happen often and the old man knew he ought to make the most of it. But what kind of man-to-man talk could he initiate that wouldn't drive the boy into a sullen silence?

Right now, though they walked without speaking, the boy didn't *seem* sullen.

The subject the old man *wanted* them to talk about was the boy's relationship with this Mandy, their new "house guest." But what could he ask that wouldn't sound like a third-degree?

And what were first and second degree interrogations anyway? Maybe... gentler, like degrees of being burned?

You never heard about them on cop shows, back in the day. The boy would never have seen any cop shows. Growing into his teenaged years without television...? Who'd ever have guessed that would come around again?

The man and boy were on the foodbank run so that the woman and girl could talk.

Being on the streets in the gray half-empty city center always felt uncertain. Better to wander the alleys if there was reason to go out. But the foodbank wasn't in an alley.

They walked most of the way side-by-side without speaking, but pointing out other pedestrians and together crossing streets to avoid them. However as they approached the old converted church, the boy suddenly said, "She's nice, isn't she?"

"She seems nice," the old man said. It was as close to agreeing as he could manage. Who knew what Mandy was really like, who she was, even what she was. That's what he hoped his daughter was using this time to learn more about.

The boy was silent again. It was not praise enough.

The sudden introduction of a new person, a complete stranger, filled the old man with anxieties. There was nothing *obviously* wrong with Mandy. She'd cleaned up well and was apparently healthy. She knew how to behave. But...

"I just don't know her," the old man said. For the boy he added, "Yet."

That helped, though the boy said nothing more.

But a new mouth to feed? A stranger among them, one with no ID card or legitimate way to contribute to their supplies?

Though thin and basically small, Mandy had already eaten as if she'd never eaten before. Well, maybe she was starving, if she'd been out on her own for weeks. If what little of her story she'd told them so far could be believed.

And then the boy had found her. Or she had found the boy.

"We need more information," the old man's daughter had said. "I need to talk to her without your grandson hovering over her shoulder."

But the boy had worried about leaving Mandy, fearful she'd be gone when he got back.

"No one's going anywhere," the boy's mother had told him in a firm voice. And with that reassurance the boy and his grandfather set out for the foodbank.

*

"Next!"

They were called in by a short, broad woman.

Only people who worked in foodbanks could grow fat these days, the old man thought as they walked forward. He'd never been fat but his aunt had a fat brother. "It's my metabolism," Fat Uncle Aaron had explained. "My genes."

Genes or greed, Fat Uncle Aaron had died back in the first wave.

The old man presented the family ID cards. And they were lucky. The large woman counted out various cans, packages and three loaves of bread. "No winter clothes today," she said. "Maybe next time."

Then, surprisingly, the boy spoke. "Is there any dogfood, please?" He smiled shyly at the woman.

"You have a dog?" she said. "You haven't eaten it?"

The old man's heart sank: would she take some of their allowance back?

But the boy said, "Oh no! I could never do that." He smiled again and added, gently, "My dog is lovely. I hate when she's still hungry even after I've shared my food with her. She's my best friend." He turned away and rubbed his eyes, though one wasn't supposed to rub one's eyes, even with gloves on.

The woman was silent, staring at him. Then she laughed unexpectedly. "You're good at this," she said. She left the trestle table and returned with six cans. "Don't eat them all at once," and she helped the boy load the dogfood into his backpack. "I hear it makes good sandwiches." She laughed again.

For just a second the boy looked offended. Then he too laughed. Something had changed. The woman glanced around to see whether anyone from another table was paying attention to them, but even the Buttons assigned to the bank seemed to be dozing in his chair.

"Here," the woman said after reaching below her table. She slipped a bar of chocolate into the boy's backpack alongside the cans.

"Thank you!" he said, clearly thrilled.

And it seemed to the old man that the woman wanted to pat his grandson's cheek. The boy's got charm, he thought. He'd never thought that before.

The Buttons snorted and turned, but he didn't seem to wake up.

The woman said sharply, "Now off with you. Next!" But she winked.

*

"Chocolate!" the boy said when they were out of anyone's earshot.

"Probably," the old man said.

"It sure looked like a chocolate bar to me."

They were silent again, walking quickly. The old man wondered if his grandson was thinking about chocolate rather than the girl.

Apart from the boy's birthday cupcake no one in the family had tasted chocolate for… The old man had lost count of the time. No television, no chocolate… This had been the boy's life for years.

The candy bar was bound to be out of date, but even so. His having it was a minor miracle and not just of chocolate, but of human connection with the woman at the foodbank.

Back in the day the old man's favorite was a Clark Bar, chocolate wrapped around some chewy stuff with honey and peanuts.

He'd had a paper route for nearly a year and he saved enough from what he gave Auntie to spend a dime on chocolate most every day.

A dime… When was the last time he'd seen a dime? The most common one in his newspaper days had

FDR's profile on one side. Would the boy or even his daughter remember who FDR was?

They couldn't half use an FDR now...

*

When they got home, the boy rushed in. Pansy Valiant ran to greet him, standing on her hind legs and stretching up to lick his face.

But the boy was scanning the room.

"They're probably upstairs," the old man said. "Your mom's coat is still here. They haven't gone out." Then, "I'm sure the girl's here too."

"She better be," the boy said.

Did he fear he'd been tricked? Sent out so that something he loved could be disposed of?

That happened to a kid in the old man's high school. A beloved dog had been put down while Terry was at school one day – his parents said the dog had run away.

Sniffy – the old man remembered the dog's name – had chewed the legs of their furniture. That was its death sentence.

Terry went mad.

He'd shot his father with a gun he found in the house by his mother's bed. Didn't kill him, but it got Terry sent away too.

Was his grandson capable of doing something like *that* if he felt betrayed. The old man looked to the corner where they kept their two guns.

Mandy *was* still here, wasn't she?

He and the boy unpacked the groceries in silence. Even putting out the chocolate bar didn't seem to cheer the boy up.

It *was* nearly a year out of date, but that didn't really matter for chocolate. Did it?

Finally the old man's daughter came down from the rooms above. "How'd you do?" she asked. "Any problems?"

"Your boy charmed them out of dog food and a chocolate bar."

"No!" She went to hug her son but he stepped back.

"Where is she?"

"Upstairs."

He took two stairs at a time as he ran up.

"Shall we have a hot drink?" the boy's mother asked. She took the pan off a shelf and ran some water in it.

The old man got out the camping stove and its current gas cylinder. "And?" he asked.

"It's OK, Pa."

"You're sure?"

"She comes from a farm, up the river."

"A *farm*?"

"She ran away. She's been on her own nearly two weeks. She hid until sunset, then tried to find things to eat in the dark. Pansy Valiant spotted her in an alley one evening."

But the old man was stuck on the farm. "They always have food on farms, don't they? Is she crazy?" Mandy had looked kind of crazy when she first came in, and then she would hardly talk to them. She probably talked with the boy upstairs. But then *he* hadn't talked with them.

"She's not crazy, Pa," his daughter said.

He measured coffee into cups, poured the hot water and stirred. He gave a cup to his daughter.

"They wanted her to get pregnant."

"They *what*?"

"Her older sisters are pregnant. They've got these ideas about richies paying a lot of money for babies. Part of trying to repopulate… Or if not for that then because they'll need workers." His daughter shrugged. "Mandy says it was like breeding animals. She's thirteen, Pa."

The old man couldn't think of a word extreme enough for what he felt. But then he frowned, and asked, "And?"

"She doesn't think she's pregnant."

"Doesn't think?"

"Starvation, and anxiety, they can stop periods."

He'd heard that.

"She'd have to have been very unlucky," his daughter said.

"But girls can have bad luck," the old man said.

"They certainly can," she said with a frown.

14. VISION

The old man chose a main street for his climb up the hill – a street he knew from years before.

Back then a public park was at the top. It had a panoramic vista over the city. It also had sandboxes and playground equipment for children. He'd taken his daughter there when she was young.

But was it still a park? Was it still "public"? And what *would* he see if he got that far?

Maybe the journey would be like going back in time the way it was in the old days when you traveled to a rural town. He'd had a selling job once and visited distant places where town centers looked frozen in the past – buildings made of wood and no taller than two stories. There were stores with loose candy to scoop into bags, and tables in little restaurants covered with polkadot oilcloth.

If life up the hill did take him back in time it wouldn't be anything like that. But would he find crowds of cars and sidewalks packed with people? Stores with full shelves? Coffee shops, bars, places to buy bright clothes?

Maybe, just maybe, the richies still lived the kind of life that everybody had before the virus.

Was that *possible*?

*

He wasn't far up the incline when differences from the city center began to show. Most dramatic was the frequency of security measures. Windows and doors that were barred and some houses surrounded by link fences topped by electric wiring.

What were they afraid of? Strangers – people like *him* – who would break in to steal and… whatever?

As he climbed farther the old man surprised himself by picturing a cherry pie cooling on the sill of an open window, just begging to be stolen the way it happened in old movies and cartoons…

It was a stupid image, given the barred windows and cold weather. But if he did see such a thing he might be tempted to become one of the scary marauding *strangers…*

But that's not why he was heading up the hill, taking the risk of going where he so obviously didn't belong.

*

The first commercial premises he came to were a small food market next to a drugstore, about halfway up. Although he was across the street from them, he could see a Buttons inside each entrance.

Two cars were parked outside – the first cars he'd seen, though he'd been passed by a few pick-ups. Both cars were old but noticeably clean and shiny.

It made sense that richies – or even near-richies, if that's who shopped this low – would take good care of cars that were unlikely to be replaceable. Were any *new* cars being produced now? He'd never seen one while walking in the city center.

He began to struggle with his breathing – had he been climbing too quickly? He slowed, but carried on.

And then, as the street took a bend, he saw what he'd expected to find at some point: a barrier blocking the way for pedestrians and vehicles alike.

Metal huts on each side were part of the structure. It reminded the old man of the gates outside military bases. Like cooling cherry pies, he'd mostly seen such things in movies but he'd been to an airforce base once as part of a crew catering for a party there. His boss had all the right paperwork but everyone still had to get out of their minivan to be studied and searched. Like what happened whenever he ran into a Buttons now.

Just short of the hut on his side he stopped and bent over, wanting to catch his breath. But before he moved on two Buttons left the hut to meet him, one man and one woman.

We're off and running, the old man thought.

The male Buttons said, "Problem, old timer?" as he took the old man's temperature.

"Just… just finding it hard to catch my breath."

"ID," the woman said.

The old man held his ID up, having been ready for the instruction. The woman waved a scanner over it and turned away.

The male Buttons said, "Any pain, like in your chest or arm?"

As if I would have medical coverage, the old man thought. "No. No. Just..." He gasped, making more sound than necessary.

"You been tested?"

"Not today."

"Hold out your hand."

The old man offered a hand and the Buttons put on gloves and withdrew a kit from a pocket. The test involved puncturing a finger. The Buttons got the required blood quickly.

The result would show up in a couple of minutes, but the old man said, "I got lung problems. I'm sure I don't got the sickness. But it's always good to test."

The Buttons nodded and stepped back.

The woman Buttons approached. "No address," she said. "What are you doing here?"

"Looking for my mom."

She frowned, as did the male Buttons who'd overheard. "Your mom?"

"Her house is around here someplace." The old man waved vaguely in the direction beyond the barrier. "My room's upstairs, next to the bathroom."

"What's your address?"

"I..." He shook his head. "I don't recall just at the minute."

"You *sure* you live around here?" the man said, looking the old man up and down. He gave his head a little shake.

"I always used to," the old man said. "Have *you* seen my mom's house?"

"*Me?*" The male Buttons moved away to whisper to the woman.

"It's near a park," the old man said. "*The* park. Top of the hill park. I forget its name but I'm sure it's not far." The old man pointed again beyond the barrier. "I used to take my little girl there. The sandboxes was what she loved – making cakes and castles, you know? She liked the swings too, back in the day. But things have changed so much." The old man shook his head vigorously. "I don't understand why things gotta change so much. Course, my girl's not so little now, and her mother's dead. In one of the waves. You know the waves? Terrible things." More head shaking.

"Yeah," the male Buttons said, glancing at a machine he held that had beeped. "You test negative."

"Told you I don't got it. My wife got it, got it bad. Worst day of my life." And it had been. The old man began to cry.

"Hey, hey," the male Buttons said, seeming uncertain what to do next. "Do you really not remember your address?"

"My wife would of remembered it but I was never that good with numbers, y'know? Even though I did have some selling jobs where I had to count up. But when I get to the park, I'll recognize it for sure. I always do. It isn't far." He gazed into the distance. "Is the park far?"

"I don't want to leave you alone on the street," the man said.

"Oh for cryin' out loud, Hank," the woman said. "You know it's going to come back that he belongs somewhere in the city and he's just come up here to see what he can steal."

"You looking to steal something, old timer?" the male Buttons asked.

"Me? Gosh no." He raised his hands. "Search me. I got nothing that don't belong to me. That's just wrong. You want me to show you my pockets?"

The man turned again to his colleague. "He could be someone's father, got out, they don't know where he is."

"Does he *look* like somebody's father?"

They both studied the old man. He was as spruced up as he could manage.

"Do *you* know where my house is?" the old man asked the woman. "I'm getting real tired. I want to go to my house. I want to go *home*."

"No name tag or address pinned to his lapel?" she asked the male Buttons.

He shook his head, but did not touch the old man. "What say we give him a lift to the park. Then spin back up there after half an hour, see if he's still lost."

The woman scowled but said nothing.

The male Buttons returned to the old man. "That sound OK by you, old timer? We'll take you to the park. You look around for your house. We'll come back, in case you don't find it."

"So I get to ride in your *car*?" the old man said.

*

"You rode in a Buttons' *car*, Pa?" his daughter said later when the old man reported on his expedition.

"In the back seat, behind the wire mesh. It was like a cage. And it stank."

She turned to her son and Mandy. "I can't remember the last time I rode in *any* car."

"We have cars – well, trucks – on the farm," Mandy said.

"And you rode in them?"

"Well, not really. Not us girls." She dropped her head and moved a little closer to the boy.

"You wouldn't believe how different it is up there now," the old man said.

"How?" his daughter asked. "You want more hot water in that coffee?" Not waiting for a response she topped up his mug.

"I was expecting life the way it used to be but it's *empty*, that's what it is. No one on sidewalks, no moms with their kids in the park. Not many cars on the streets or even parked. But the most amazing thing was that some of the houses – big ones – had bubble domes over them. Like they didn't even want to share the air with us."

"They're scared," Mandy said.

The adults turned to her.

"That's what my father and mother say."

They waited.

"We make deliveries from the farm. Food, to houses and to the stores."

"I did see a grocery market while I was walking around the park, trying to get different views," the old man said. "It's way bigger than anything left in the city. Buttons on the door, of course, but the prices in the window! Astronomical."

"Is that because supplies of a lot of things are limited?" his daughter asked. But she shrugged, not really caring. It wasn't as if they'd ever go shopping there.

"How long were you in the park, Grandpa?" the boy asked.

"Only thirty-five minutes. I tried to avoid the Buttons but the place was so empty they found me, easy."

"And?"

"I cried and said I lived down the hill after all. They couldn't be bothered to arrest me. What were they gonna do? Give me a warm place to stay and regular food? Must be hundreds trying to get that. So they drove me halfway and let me out. Stayed long enough to see that I was headed to down rather than up again."

"Seeming to be a doddery old man comes easy for you, Grandpa," the boy said with a smile, but then he looked quickly to Mandy.

She gave a little shake of the head. Disrespecting his grandfather? Mandy's manners were, so far, faultless.

"So, Pa," the old man's daughter asked, "what did you *see*?"

"I saw the river good, all the way up and down and even the stretch near the foodbank. It's not entirely clogged up with branches and other stuff, but it looks worst near the bridges."

"And?"

"I didn't see a single boat."

"Oh," his daughter said. The children looked at each other.

"Much less one we might "borrow". Not a single damn boat. So we're going to have to think of some other way to get out of here."

15. PEACHES

"Should we be worried?" The old man *was* worried but at this point his daughter knew Mandy, and the young people's relationship, better than he did.

The new addition to their family didn't talk much around him – was it because he was male? – but now she did talk sometimes to his daughter. Who shared the information. Most important was that Mandy feared that her parents would be looking for her.

But this day the thirteen-year-old had ventured out, with the boy and Pansy Valiant. And now they'd been gone nearly an hour. Was he silly to worry? Too protective? But *could* one be too protective nowadays? The old man shook his head.

"They've had the talk, Pa," his daughter said when she turned from organizing their food supplies.

"The talk?" The old man furrowed his brow. Did she mean sex?

But seeing his daughter's smile he said, "Oh lordie. *The* talk?"

"To keep away from people, wear masks, look over their shoulders. Your grandson knows it all backwards, but it was good to go through it again for Mandy. And if she was living on her own for as long as she says, she'll know how to keep safe."

Should they worry about sex too, even though they were so young? The truth was he hadn't thought about that at all, despite the fact that the boy and Mandy spent a lot of time together upstairs.

He'd been more concerned about her skittishness around him. But at least she'd become more outgoing when the family was together. Enough to have said suddenly the previous day, "You won't turn me in, will you?"

"Turn you in?" the old man had said. "Who to?"

"The Buttons. My parents will probably offer a reward for me."

The old man had been shocked.

But his daughter had said, "Of course not. Of *course* we won't turn you in to them or anybody else."

"I told you," the boy had said.

And the old man had added his agreement.

Now as he returned to stretching damp clothes before putting them on their clothesline he wondered if the boy would even know how to do sex?

Should they have a sex talk? Lordie.

His own mother had spoken bitterly about men. "They treat us like playthings. Not as if we're people like them. And you'll be a man soon too," she'd told her six-year-old son. "Before you know it. God, I hope you turn out different."

That was all the sex talk he got.

When the old man was twelve a classmate brought a girlie magazine to school to show off. The few glances he got before it was confiscated had helped with anatomical basics. *That's* what women looked like? Nipples didn't both point forward like his did? Hair *there*?

Back in the day such publications still showed pictures of women with pubic hair. Would his grandson's the first experience of a real life nude woman surprise him even more these days?

Constructive sexual education had waited until the old man was married. Women could come too? Wow.

"How long have they been gone, Pa?" his daughter asked.

He looked at his watch. "Nearly an hour and a quarter now."

"I wish they'd come home," she said quietly. "They're in the target group."

The safety talk necessarily included scary stories about hijackers who snatched the young and the fit for forced labor. Such stories first appeared when it became clear how serious the disease was. There would be a shortage of pickers for fruit and vegetables.

Were the stories true? They *might* be. After all, the old man once had a guy try to lure him to the riverbank.

But the old man's daughter moved on to a new thought. "What if Mandy's folks *are* out there looking for her. For messing up their breeding program, or just because she's their valuable property. Would she be some official kind of missing person or would they send their own people out to try to reconstruct her trail?"

It was the old man's turn to offer reassurance. "The children know the dangers, love. And we couldn't keep them locked up here if we tried."

"I just hope they pay attention to more than each other." His daughter stood and picked up her jacket. "I need to go to the foodbank, Pa."

He looked at his watch again. "Yeah." Then, "I'll come with you."

"Sure?" They rarely left their "home" completely unattended. Not that having someone in the place would make it secure against anyone bigger and stronger who really wanted it.

"They'll be back soon," he said. "And maybe you'll be lucky and need help carrying everything."

"Because a truckful of fresh fruit and vegetables just came in?"

It had been a long time since they'd had anything fresh. "What would you give for an apple or an orange?" he asked.

"I'd give my brightest, shiniest smile," she said.

*

The old man wasn't allowed in with her. He used the time to walk around the recycled church. There was no point heading down to the river – he'd had a good view of that from the park up the hill. But he'd never examined what was behind the foodbank.

It turned out to be an abandoned middle school – a long, flat, brick building with its windows knocked out. Slowly he walked around it. There were remains of police tape that had closed it as a recognized center of infection. Not that he had any inclination to go inside anyway. For all he knew it was now the "home" of people even more desperate than he and his family were.

On the other side he found a rectangle of asphalt peppered with weeds that had pushed their way through, determined to live, craving light. He checked them for anything edible, like dandelions. That was as close to fresh produce as they got these days. Not that his grandson had yet been persuaded to eat dandelions, despite being ready to down almost anything else. "Too bitter," he said. "More for us," was his mother's retort.

In fact every bit of a dandelion was edible. Hadn't he heard that somewhere?

But he didn't see anything that looked familiar.

Near the edges of the formerly paved areas were a couple of metal basketball backboards, missing their hoops.

Basketball. He'd enjoyed playing that in the park with friends, back in the day. Set their jackets and any bags they were carrying at courtside and lose themselves in half-court games. Good times.

He glanced at his watch, and headed back toward the foodbank entrance area.

It was a pity about the river. Rivers joined up to flow south and to warmer places. It was an idea. A dream?

But in fact the only thing that kept them alive here in the city was the foodbank. Which was still being supplied, if inconsistently, from god knew where. Canned and plastic-wrapped foodstuffs, supplemented sometimes with clothing. Was it the product of what remained of government? Or just richies' charity?

So many questions, and no neighbors or TV or radio or internet news to answer them.

Were there *really* people lurking in dark corners who might snatch his grandson and Mandy? Or take Pansy Valiant for food?

They'd been lucky with Pansy Valiant, who never strayed far from their protection. And like the humans in the family, she seemed healthy.

What would any of them would do if they got sick? The one time he'd walked past a clinic there was a line outside that stretched around the block. And he didn't know of any hospitals that were open.

Could Mandy be pregnant? Was that still a possibility? He'd ask his daughter.

He was drawn from his musings when she emerged and said, "Good news, Pa."

"What?"

"Fruit salad today!"

"Really? You'll be able to make a fruit salad?" His wife's fruit salads had been one of the things she made that he loved best.

"Get real." His daughter held up a can that said Fruit Salad on the label.

*

The yarn store was empty when the old man and his daughter returned from the foodbank. Now he was really worried.

But the adults hadn't finished unpacking when the two young people burst in. Pansy Valiant overtook them and leapt on the old man with pleasure. He buried his face in her fur to hide his tears of relief.

"Mom, Grandpa, look!" the boy said, noticing nothing.

"What?" The old man raised his head.

The boy displayed a plastic bag of peaches.

"Fresh fruit!" the boy said.

"But... how? Where?" the old man said. His daughter was examining the bag, her brightest, shiniest smile on her face.

"It's not like they grows on trees," the boy said, as if he'd rehearsed the joke for them.

"We bought them," Mandy said, shy and proud.

"Mandy has money!" the boy said.

16. TOOLS

The old man was angry. With his grandson. With Mandy. With the *world*. He didn't know what he was angriest about. "I'm going to look for some tools," he declared and grabbed his jacket.

The children were upstairs, and obviously confused, but his daughter just wished him luck: she understood that he had to get out.

So he got out, and walked.

And walked some more.

Yes, with the idea that having some tools could help them, help *him*. But his mind was all over the place. Filled with anger.

And yes, he was supposed to keep alert about his own safety. Blah blah.

But he didn't fucking care. If the kids wanted to screw up, let them screw up. If the collectors wanted to hijack him for farm labor, fine.

He hadn't taken Pansy Valiant, though she'd run to the door with him and wagged her tail and whined.

Not interested.

He'd almost refused to wear his mask. But, pissed off or not, as soon as he got out the door he'd been hit with the fact that there *was* still the world to deal with. Sickness. Strangers. Buttons. Scavengers.

Well, he'd be a scavenger too. What he wanted most to find was a hammer somewhere. Ooo, wouldn't it feel good to *hit* something. He could *feel* the weight of his old steel hammer in his hand. The rubber grip, the satisfaction of walloping a nail really hard; driving it home with a single blow.

He'd built a lot of things around the house when he and his wife still thought life could be more than just a struggle for survival. Shelves, even cabinets. He'd grown good with wood, though he'd never been taught as a child. And the more he'd built the better he got at it.

His wife was always encouraging. He recognized that when he re-examined what he'd built as his very first project. Just shelves to fill an alcove, but not quite right. Yet she hadn't said so. She'd loved that he'd made something and that it worked well enough.

He missed her so much. He missed the hell out of her. He'd give his right arm to have her to talk with now. Sometimes he felt as if he *had* given his right arm. Her death still felt like an amputation. Oh, love, what should I do…?

Not realizing he'd stopped, he began walking again.

"I try my damnedest to protect them!" he shouted to the empty street. "What more do you want?" To hell with whoever might hear him, might be drawn by the sound.

The fucking "new" world. He hated how it made him ineffective, and stupid, and powerless.

He walked more quickly.

Feeling angry was hardly a novelty, but he rarely expressed his full furies. Even as a child. Even when his mother and Plum died.

But once, oh yes… He was seven-years-old, fostered and going to school. He couldn't recall what set things off but his teacher had opened the flap of his desk and said, "No no. We're not having that."

Not having what? He could close the lid if he pressed down hard. And everything inside was important.

But this teacher brought a wastepaper basket from beside her desk, plonked it down, and began throwing his possessions away.

The dog collar he kept in case he ever owned a dog, the jar with his collection of dead spiders, the candy bar wrappers that still smelled of chocolate…

"No!" screamed the seven-year-old. And he pushed the teacher all the way from the back of the classroom and up against the blackboard at the front. Fury made him strong.

Throwing away his *stuff*? *His* stuff? All the things he wasn't allowed to keep in his foster "home" – the rattle that had been Plum's favorite, the scarf that smelled of his mother, the pretty leaves, the stones that might be pieces of arrowheads, the skull of a dead bird, the box

125

from a toy car Eddie, the boy next door, bought with his pocket money…

He'd really wanted the car itself, but the box was better than nothing. Maybe one day it would magically fill itself: there was no chance if he didn't keep the box.

He was not about to lose any of it to some damn wastebasket. To some damn teacher.

The old man didn't remember how the classroom part of the drama had ended. But later he was taken to be punished by the school's principal. His foster mother, wearing her mink coat, came to the meeting.

He remembered the coat but he couldn't remember his punishment. Yet what was it for? Roughing up a teacher? She'd *taken* his *things*! Shouldn't *she* be taught that stealing was *wrong*?

Just make sure *she* never does it again, he hoped he had said after the stern and threatening ruler was waved in his face.

The old man did not spend much longer in that foster home. Maybe he'd been labeled as "violent". He didn't know. But he felt now as ultimately powerless as he had been at seven.

All he could do was scream.

The boy and Mandy had gone into a store and spent *money*. They risked the safety of the whole family. Couldn't they *see* that?

"You don't just spend money without thinking it through," he'd told them, though mostly addressing the boy.

"But Mom did," the boy had said.

"That was her own money, not Mandy's, and we knew where it came from."

"It came from Mandy," the boy said.

"I brought it with me," Mandy said. "He didn't steal it or anything."

"But where did *you* get it?" the old man said. "And what store did you go in? Who saw you? And who followed you after you came out?" He'd jerked a thumb toward his daughter. "When your Mom bought things we talked it through ahead of time. All the possible dangers."

"You didn't talk about it with me," the boy said stubbornly.

"Because it was a surprise for your birthday. We wanted to do something special when you turned fifteen."

"This was supposed to be a surprise for you and Mom," the boy said. "Mandy wanted to thank you for taking her in." He was near tears.

The boy's mother tried to intervene and calm the rising level of anger between her son and her father. "Where did you spend the money?" she asked the young people.

"In that store we robbed before we moved here," the boy said. "I saw then they had some fresh fruit."

"Who handed the money over?"

"*I* did, Mom. I'm not stupid. I knew they'd ID me. And Mandy stayed outside. We were careful. If their security cameras were working I'm the only one they saw."

That *had* shown some thought. "Good," his mother said. She turned to Mandy. "Tell me about the money, will you?"

"It's mine," Mandy said, but she hid herself behind the boy.

"I'm not thinking of taking it away from you or anything like that, love," the old man's daughter said. "But, for instance, is it notes or coins?"

"Notes. They were easier to carry. But a few coins now, from the change."

"So you took what you could find when you left the farm?"

A nod.

"I'm trying to get an idea whether there'd be any way your folks might be alerted that some of their money was spent in a store. Like if it was marked somehow."

"I... I don't think so." She turned to the boy, who shrugged.

The old man's daughter said, "How did your parents deal with cash money they got? Did they take pictures of notes they handled, for the serial numbers?"

"I don't know about anything like that," the girl said quietly.

"Do you have any left?"

"Yes, ma'am."

"May I see it?"

"What I've got on me or what I hid?"

She'd hidden some? More news. But the old man's daughter said, "What you've got now."

Mandy turned away and brought out some notes and a few coins from somewhere in her clothing.

The adults each examined the notes. There were three twenty-dollar bills and a ten. "I don't see anything, Pa," the old man's daughter said.

"Me neither. But I guess it could still be marked in a way that only shows under ultraviolet."

They gave the cash back to Mandy.

"It's a matter of safety," the boy's mother said. "Because you said your folks might be looking for you."

The girl dropped her head and said nothing. The posture and silence reminded the old man of her first days with them.

"They'll want her back," the boy said. "Of course they will. She's valuable to them."

This was the first time Mandy's potential danger to them all had been spoken aloud. What if her parents found her in the old yarn store? Would they just ask her please to come home? Or would they truss her up and then kill everyone who'd harbored her? It was scary and ugly to contemplate the uncertainties.

"At least you didn't go to the store nearby," the old man's daughter said.

"No, ma'am," Mandy said.

"But you can't just go out and spend money because you feel like it. Do both you get that?"

"Were you followed?" the old man asked abruptly. "Was there anyone hanging around near the store? Did you even bother to check?"

"You take us for idiots," the boy shouted. "But we're not." He jumped up, obviously sick of the cross-examination, and the disapproval.

"Come on," his mother said. "Let's have some peaches."

"The peaches can go rot," the boy said. "We wanted to do a nice thing but you've gone and spoiled it. I hate you. I hate everything!" He took Mandy by the hand and led her upstairs.

After some silence, the old man's daughter had said, "Pa?"

"Everything I've tried to do. All at risk for some peaches."

The old man had stormed out. He couldn't just sit there. He had to *do* something. That's what being responsible for other people's safety meant.

And now he found himself in an alley that ran between the backyards of two rows of houses and he didn't remember how he'd gotten there. He was a long way from home. His chest heaved and his vision was blurry. That was because he'd walked too far too fast, right?

He stood, panting and rubbing his eyes with raw knuckles.

How had his knuckles become scraped? He didn't remember.

What he *wanted* was to get out, to get his little family out. But if they couldn't do that, then he had to make them all safer where they were. Build stronger walls, stronger doors… They were his "stuff".

A man's home is his castle, right? He wanted turrets, a drawbridge. He could build them, once he decided what was best.

But he'd need tools.

He peered through some rotten fencing and just saw a yard choked with bindweed. Even the fencing was too crumbly to make anything with.

He felt old, and crumbly himself. Would the story of his life end as it had begun: losing things, and people, he couldn't bear to lose?

17. MAN AND BOY

When the old man finally returned to the yarn store he found his daughter sitting on the floor, leaning against a wall, head in her hands.

And doing nothing.

But she was always doing something. "Love?" he asked, going to her. "What's wrong?"

She looked up at him and took some gulping breaths. "They're gone, Pa," she said.

He eased himself to the floor, facing her. "What?" He didn't grasp what she was saying.

"While you were out, my son… He came downstairs and put a leash on Pansy Valiant and he said, 'I need to walk her.' He put his mask on but when he got to the door he turned and said, 'Look, no backpack.' I didn't understand why he said that so I just said, 'Be careful.' But he never came back."

The old man couldn't take it in. He looked at his watch. It was after nine. How long had he been out himself? "When did he leave?"

"I don't know," she said, shaking her head. "Hours. Does it matter how long?"

"Of course not," the old man said gently. He sat and pulled her close.

"I gave it a while after he and Pansy Valiant left and then I went upstairs. I thought maybe I could talk with Mandy. Calm things down. But she wasn't there."

"How…?"

"Out the window. Their backpacks, their clothes, his sleeping bag and her blankets, all gone. She must've jumped. He'd have waited underneath to catch things and then help break her fall. They've *left* us, Pa." She pressed her face against his chest and sobbed. "I didn't know what to do. You weren't here. I was scared something had happened to you too." Tears that had been leaking now flooded. The old man's daughter's cried harder than he could remember her ever crying.

He held her, kissed her hair. What use would it be for him to say, "I'm here now. It's OK." None. Because it wasn't OK. And he wanted to cry himself. *Gone*? His grandson…?

"They'll be caught," she said. "I just know it. They'll be taken. I'll never see him again."

"You will if I have anything to do about it."

She snorted, and he recognized the emptiness of his words. But then he said, "You've got to remember, he's not stupid."

"No," she whispered after a pause.

"He's aware of all the risks. He's grown up hearing about them, every day."

"Yes," with a snuffle.

"And now he'll feel he's responsible for Mandy and Pansy Valiant. It's like he's head of a new family and he won't be slow to realize that if something goes wrong, it'll be his fault. He'll hate the very idea of that – like I do. He'll be more careful than ever."

His daughter's silence was progress. But the old man felt a stab of exactly the kind of failed responsibility he'd referred to.

"I see that," she said after wiping her nose on a sleeve.

So the old man *had* been able to help her, by reminding her how capable her son was, even if he'd committed a rash act.

But how rash was it?

Had his grandson behaved like a petulant teenager or had he decided to take on responsibility like that of a grown man with a girl and dog to care for? After all he'd *found* Mandy: rescued her and made her feel safe again. Well, safer.

Until those damn peaches.

The boy had felt his grandfather's fury at the peaches as a personal attack, just when he was maybe beginning to feel like an adult. The old man's sense of responsibility had undermined his grandson's. And in front of both Mandy and his mother.

Yet, the old man thought, what else could he have done? He'd only been trying to protect them *all*. He felt mixed up and misunderstood. As, he supposed, the boy must have felt.

If he ever got his grandson back, he would work to treat him as more of an equal. The boy was fifteen now, after all.

Fifteen… Back in the day that was hardly a significant age. He'd have been a sophomore in high school, playing ball with friends after classes, showing off to girls on a skateboard. But his grandson had not had a child's life – with its unconcern for where food came from, and its default sense of security.

It was a different world now. The one his grandson had grown up in.

After a while he said, "Your mother was good in a crisis. What do you think she might have done about this?"

His daughter took a moment to consider. "Mom would think about food. What will they eat?"

He gave a chuckle and she chimed in. But he said, "So let's think about food."

Together they examined their supplies. Nothing was missing or appeared to have been disturbed.

Which was no surprise. His daughter said, "They would have decided to leave suddenly. They couldn't come down to get anything because that would have shown what they were planning. So will they go to a store? Spend *more* money?"

"Maybe," the old man said, "peaches weren't the only thing they bought."

His daughter tilted her head. "Ah."

"If you were a kid, and went into a store with more money than you'd *ever* had before would you buy fresh peaches for your mother and grandfather and nothing for yourself?"

She laughed, though her nose was blocked and it sounded more like a snort. "I get it. Candy, if there was any. Or cookies, or…"

"Could be anything. So probably they're not going to starve tonight."

"Just freeze?"

"Not with the sleeping bag and blankets. And remember, Mandy found places to sleep before she came here. She didn't freeze, or get caught."

"True."

Then suddenly the old man got up. He went to the corner where they hid their guns.

"Pa?"

"Both still there," he said with relief. He turned back to her. "So where might they go?"

The old man thought of the abandoned middle school. Not *there*, surely. But then he had a different idea.

*

The boy and Mandy were pressed against a wall, their postures defensive. The boy held a dark object – the old man couldn't see what in the dim light, though it wasn't one of the guns.

However Pansy Valiant knew who the surprise visitors were and immediately ran to greet them. She leapt on the old man and licked his face as he bent to greet her too. "It's going to be all right," he said to the dog.

Then a flashlight illuminated the newcomers. They'd had a flashlight upstairs at the yarn store, of course they did. The boy said, "We're not coming back."

"You'll do whatever you think is best," the old man said as he straightened.

"How did you know we were here?"

"You'd want to be indoors overnight if you could. We used to live here so you knew where it was. I'm glad it's still empty."

The boy's mother said, "We brought you some things that might help." She began to unload cans from her backpack. "Food for you two and dogfood for Pansy Valiant."

The old man unloaded the camping stove and cans of fuel from his own backpack.

"We don't need all that," the boy said sharply.

"We have money," Mandy said.

"It's just until you get registered at the foodbank in your own name," the boy's mother said. "You still can't know for sure whether it's safe to use that money."

"And it's probably not good to buy things over and over from the same store," the old man said. "If an owner or a black-marketeer thinks you have a lot of cash they might follow you and rob you. Or worse."

The boy was silent. The adults continued to unload what they'd brought.

When their backpacks were empty they prepared to leave. There was an awkward silence. Then, timidly, Mandy said, "Thank you."

"That'll see you through for a few days," the old man's daughter said. "Better for you to have it all now anyway, since Mandy's pregnant."

*

"Do you think he realized about her?" the old man said as they headed back toward the yarn store.

"I don't think even she's sure," his daughter said. "What can she know about how it would affect her body? But she is gaining weight – on what *we* could feed her? And…"

"And what?"

"Yesterday she asked me if we ever have any fish sticks."

"What on earth makes her think we'd have fish sticks? Nobody can deal with frozen food anymore."

"She wasn't thinking logically, Pa," his daughter said sadly. "It was a craving."

18. DEAD OR ALIVE

The old man felt a real need to accompany his daughter to their next foodbank appointment. Not because he believed she was at any new risk, but having lost his grandson all the old risks loomed larger. "I just don't want you out of my sight," he explained as he went to get his jacket too. "Not now."

"I get that, Pa," she said. "I wouldn't want you out alone either."

Then, as they bundled up, he said, "Is it too early to think about what we do when Mandy has her baby?"

"We?"

"Oh, come on. They won't want to go through that alone, not when you could help them."

"If they're still around, you mean? If they're even speaking to us?"

"Don't talk like that. I'm not letting them go – or giving up on them – any more than you are."

The old man's daughter took a deep breath, and nodded. "It's just so hard for me to think anything good, Pa."

"I get that, love. But he knows how much we care, and he'll want what's best for Mandy too."

The old man's daughter said, "It'll be up to her, I guess, when she thinks through what she wants. Maybe she'll let me help, whether they live with us again or not. Though I wonder if she really believes it yet."

"And maybe I can get information from somewhere." He thought. "Or ask for a first aid kit at the foodbank?"

"It's not a disease, or an injury."

"There's blood."

"There is certainly blood," his daughter said.

They set out. And as they walked the old man thought about when his wife was in labor, the panic to get her to the hospital, the delay because he had to fill in forms. But eventually he just kissed her goodbye and only saw her again when it was time to greet his daughter. Back in the day they didn't let husbands anywhere near the actual birth.

And he hadn't minded, just accepting what he was told to do. He'd passed hours in a waiting room, eating vending machine candy, drinking vending machine coffee and watching sports on the television with three other men. They'd hardly spoken to one another.

But there would be none of that for Mandy or his grandson. There wouldn't even be a hospital.

Which made him think again about a first aid kit. Why hadn't they thought of asking for one before? What if something went wrong?

So many questions these days began with "What if…"

*

On the way to the foodbank they seemed to see Buttons ahead of them every time they turned a corner. Avoiding them made the trip longer than usual.

Then one Buttons, a woman with startlingly red hair, stopped them as they were about to cross a street. She scanned their IDs but when a radio call came in she seemed excited by it and waved them on.

But as they were nearing the church building that housed the foodbank, a lanky male Buttons stepped out of a doorway and blocked them again.

"Where are you two going?" he asked.

They both had their ID cards ready. "To the foodbank," the old man's daughter said. "But we were already scanned by one of your colleagues only a couple of minutes ago."

"Yeah?" The Buttons scanned one card, humming while he waited for the result. Then he scanned the other, continuing to hum.

The old man's daughter asked, "What's the tune?"

"What? Oh. I don't know its name," he said, looking up. "Just something my mom used to sing to me at bedtime." He laughed. "I think it was about lost love and a tragic death, but I didn't understand the words. I just liked that she was there and singing to me." He studied his screen. "So you're father and daughter?"

"That's right," the old man said.

His daughter asked, "How is your mother? Did she make it?"

"She got sick but it didn't kill her. She's never been quite the same as she was before, but a least..." He spread his hands, even though one still held the scanner.

"I lost my mom," the old man's daughter said. "So be grateful you've still got yours."

"I am." The Buttons' eyes crinkled as if he was smiling beneath his mask. Then he looked at his screen again. "You've got a son, yeah?"

"Yes."

"Well, the reason we're out in force is that we're looking for a young girl. She got lost from her family and they're really worried. Have you seen a girl, maybe thirteen, on her own? Five feet one, light brown hair? Skinny?"

"I haven't," the old man's daughter said. "Have you, Pa?"

"I hardly see anyone on the streets these days," the old man said. "How long has she been missing?"

"It's nearly a month now."

"And you think she's around here?"

"I don't know why they chose this area today." He tapped the screen on his scanner a few times, then held it up. "This is what she looks like."

The old man saw a small but recognizable picture of Mandy. He said, "My eyes ain't as good as they used to be. Yours, love?"

"She looks unhappy. Couldn't they get her to smile?"

"I dunno," the Buttons said. "I'm just stopping people and asking. But there's a reward. It'd be well worth it if you find her and let us know."

"Really?" the old man's daughter said.

"Dead or alive?" the old man said.

"Pa!"

"Well, the officer says she's been missing near a month and it's gotten damn cold." He turned to the Buttons. "Bodies get found sometimes, don't they?"

"They do," the Buttons said. "But let's try to be a bit more optimistic. You can imagine how the parents must feel."

"I wasn't trying to be a dick," the old man said. "Just asking. And I'd sure hate to lose a child." He put an arm around his daughter's shoulders.

"And then not know what's happened to her?" the Buttons said. "That must be awful."

The old man's daughter said, "You seem kind of concerned."

"We're not all hardasses, you know. And I grew up here." He gestured behind him – not pointing up the hill. "A lot of officers get brought in from bigger cities and they think this is hicksville. But I say it's a good place. Well, it used to be, y'know?"

"I appreciate your attitude," the old man said. "Mostly you guys just seem to want to scare us."

The Buttons shrugged. "They give us guidelines…" He shrugged again. Then, addressing the old man's daughter, he said, "I don't see a husband on your scan. You got someone?"

"My father and my son," she said.

"Don't think I'm being fresh, but would you like to have dinner with me sometime? There's no restaurants but my mom still makes a mean meatloaf and we probably get access to better food than you guys do." He shrugged again. "I don't make the rules."

"You're asking me on a *date*?"

"I know we only just met but you seem nice and you look great. And, tell you the truth, the women officers I meet make me want to puke, they're so aggressive and nasty. They only want to talk about how dumb the people they scan are and how boring everything is here."

"It's not a patch on what it used to be," the old man's daughter said. "There was a music scene. Like the Fountain Club? Did you ever go there? On Shelby Street? I was there a lot, but don't tell my parents." She laughed.

"Oh yeah. Great place," the Buttons said, laughing along with her. "You guys are such good decent folks. I hate hearing people like you described as dangerous and dirty. My mom's great, but it's still sad because she isn't what she used to be. I just have this feeling you might get along with her."

"I'm flattered," the old man's daughter said, "but I have so much to do keeping my own family together."

"All work and no play…?" He spread his hands again. "Although I *am* a representative of the repressive rule-bound state and you're probably afraid that if you go out with me you'd never make it back home. I've heard it all before."

"Because you ask every single woman you stop home to dinner?"

"That's not what I meant," the Buttons said with a sigh.

"I'm sorry," she said. "You do seem nice."

"I am nice," he said and he reached into a pocket, pulled out a slip of paper and gave it to her.

"What's this?"

"It's my official ID number – yup, they keep track of us too. If you change your mind, go to the officer in the foodbank – or any other – and ask them to contact me. Say you have information. They'll want to know what it is – we get bonuses for coming up with the goals they set for us, like a big one for whoever finds this missing girl."

"Do you think you'll find her?" the old man asked.

"Oh someone will find her. Or what's left of her. Where could she go and not leave a trace? Especially this time of year. Ain't no berries on the bushes, you know?" He turned back to the old man's daughter. "Tell whoever you see that you'll only talk to me. They'll let me know. We can meet outside the foodbank. OK?"

"OK," she said. "I'll think about it."

*

Once inside the foodbank the old man and his daughter spoke quietly while they waited for the supplies they'd be allotted. Meanwhile they rummaged among the cans and food packages they were allowed to pick a few from freely. "What do you think of him?" the old man asked.

"Dating? Come on, Pa."

"So you didn't like him?"

"I didn't like that there's a big reward for Mandy."

"Me neither."

"When we're done here, we need to go straight to the children and warn them."

"I agree," the old man said, a familiar knot of panic making his stomach ache. "But it's still good to know that the Buttons aren't all the same."

"You think?" his daughter said. She turned to face him. "Why did he have a slip of paper with his number on it ready in his pocket?"

The old man hadn't thought to wonder about that.

"And, Pa, there was no Fountain Club on Shelby Street."

She turned back to the crates and gathered up four cans of reconstituted beef lips.

19. DAY AND AGE

As they approached their former home, the old man and his daughter felt their anxieties growing. They'd been stopped by yet another Buttons and spotted three more of the troop sent in to search for Mandy. The children needed to be alerted, pronto.

"Oh god, Pa!" The old man's daughter ran ahead as they neared the door. When the old man caught up he saw that the latch was broken and its mounting was splintered.

His daughter began to go inside but the old man grabbed her hand.

"Wait. We don't know what's in there."

She pulled against the restraint but after a moment accepted the sense of it.

"Whatever's happened has happened. We've got to be careful," he said.

The old man didn't want to spell out what they *might* find – or think about the possibilities himself. His daughter would understand they needed to be cautious. Of course she would.

Nothing strange was visible from outside except the damage to the latch. Neither of them heard anything from inside.

Slowly they pushed the door open and eased themselves in. Exchanging the daylight for the dim interior, the old man couldn't make out anything obviously wrong.

He whistled softly. If Pansy Valiant was there, she would come running. But nothing.

"Oh Pa," his daughter said.

They went further in.

As his eyes adjusted the old man still didn't see anything wrong. Like, signs of a struggle. Or bodies...

His daughter began working her way around one wall, examining what she could in the light from the doorway.

The old man did the same on the other side, looking for any clue as to what might have happened.

When this was their home they'd never had access to the rooms above the ground floor because the stairs were missing – perhaps harvested by explorers looking for fuel rather than a place to live. But the toilet at the back had worked and was in a small room of its own.

When the old man went in it he couldn't see anything out of place. In fact he hadn't found any trace at all of his grandson or Mandy. Not even the young pair's bags and bedding; no food or equipment.

The old man and his daughter met in the middle of the room. "I've got nothing," he said. "You?"

"No."

"I don't get it," he said. "Buttons breaking in and taking them wouldn't gather up their food and clothes and sleeping things."

"Or take a dog," she said. "And it doesn't seem like people pushed them out to use the place themselves."

"Scavengers would take everything, and perhaps Pansy Valiant, but the children?"

"They might know about the money being offered for Mandy. Or that they had money – perhaps they were followed back here from a store. Oh Pa!" His daughter now grabbed the old man's arm.

The thought of his grandson and Mandy being faced by an overpowering gang of marauders left the old man shaky.

For once a part of him was glad his wife wasn't alive.

"That doesn't have to be what happened though," his daughter said suddenly.

"What do you mean?"

"Did you find any trash? Empty cans, wrapping paper? Even Pansy Valiant's bowl?"

He hadn't.

"Why would scavengers take things like that?"

Empty cans could maybe be sold but that didn't apply to all detritus. "What are you thinking?"

"Maybe they've just moved somewhere else. Maybe a place Mandy knew."

"Because... Say, they were afraid somebody followed them?"

"And they didn't feel safe here anymore?"

"That's possible." It *was* possible. The old man felt some relief. But what about the broken latch?

"We should go home, Pa. Unload what we got from the foodbank and then think what we can do next."

*

It was a good idea, but it didn't take account of running into yet another Buttons.

"Stop. The two of you, stop right there." A woman, she was as tall as the old man and powerfully built.

They stopped, found their ID cards and held them out. The old man couldn't bring himself to say anything.

"What are you up to out here?" the Buttons asked.

"We've been to the foodbank," the old man's daughter said.

"You're a long way from the foodbank." She studied one, then the other. "And why are you heading back toward it?"

"We lost our way," the old man said. He didn't sound convincing to himself, and clearly the Buttons felt the same.

She scanned them both. Then their backpacks. Her scanner responded with an ear-splitting shriek. "Empty them."

"We get cans of food," the old man said. "Of course the scanner will go off."

"Empty the goddamn sacks," the Buttons said.

Kneeling before the Buttons the old man and his daughter emptied their backpacks.

The Buttons studied the contents. "Now hold the bags up so I can see the insides."

They held their backpacks up for the Buttons to study. First she looked with a flashlight. Then she scanned the empty bags, and nothing shrieked.

"OK, I guess." She studied her scanner again. "You have a son?"

"Yes," the old man's daughter said.

"Where is he?"

"I don't know," she said with feeling. "We're looking for him. Do you know where he is?"

"What's that supposed to mean?"

"A lot of officers are patrolling around here today. If one of them picked up my son for some reason, wouldn't you be able to tell?"

"I guess I could," the Buttons said in a tone of voice that made clear there would be a month of Sundays before she did any such thing.

"Please," the old man's daughter said. "See if my son's been arrested."

The old man was horrified by the shocking but plausible idea that the boy might have done something extreme to defend Mandy or Pansy Valiant.

The Buttons just said, "No," with a smirk. "Whaddya think I am? Your search engine? Go on, get out of here. You're wasting my time."

The old man's daughter stepped forward. He felt a moment of panic – was she about to do something extreme herself? He tugged at her sleeve, but she shook him off. "Contact your colleague…" She pulled a slip of paper from her pocket and read a series of numbers.

This surprised the Buttons. "What for?"

"I have something to tell him. Information."

"What about?" When the old man's daughter didn't respond, she said, "You can tell me. We're all in it together."

"I'll only talk to him."

*

The old man and his daughter met the lanky Buttons outside the foodbank. "I'm real glad to have heard from you so soon," he said with smiling eyes. "So when you going to come to dinner?"

"I'd love to," the old man's daughter said. "The idea of real meatloaf is great. But it can't be for a while. A week or ten days."

"OK, one week," he said definitively. "I'll meet you here at five-thirty." He spoke as if the arrangement was a done deal.

The old man recognized the tone of someone used to having authority. He tried not to let his revised assessment of the apparently "nice" man to show.

"A week. I'll certainly try," the old man's daughter said. "Have you found that missing girl?"

"Not yet. If nothing turns up, they'll probably send us to a different part of the city tomorrow. But don't worry. My shifts end at five. I can make it back here by five-thirty from wherever I'll be."

"I'm glad you had time to meet us again today," the old man's daughter said then.

"Me too." His voice seemed charming, inviting.

"Because I've lost track of my son."

"Oh?"

"And I'm worried. Say, could you do me a favor? See if one of your officers has stopped him, or taken him somewhere?"

The Buttons hesitated, perhaps recognizing this was the real motivation for the meeting. But he shrugged. He was getting his dinner date. "I'll need your ID again."

When that was done he studied his machine, tapped his screen, studied it some more. "Nope. Your son's ID hasn't been scanned today."

"Thank you," the old man's daughter said brightly. "We better get on home now. But barring some emergency I'll see you here one week from today, at five-thirty."

*

The two of them headed back to their yarn store home. The old man was emotionally exhausted and so, perhaps, was his daughter.

Partly to get his mind off the prospect of her putting herself at the mercy of a Buttons on her own, he said,

"It's a real relief to know the boy hasn't been stopped today – even with all the Buttons popping out of every nook and cranny."

"Yeah, Pa."

Her tone of voice proved that his daughter was no more convinced things were all right than he was.

Suppose the boy *had* been scanned. Would the Buttons have lied just to avoid being pressed to do something? He'd sounded truthful, but they knew he was a deceitful man. Did he even have a mother?

Well, a week was a long time away. They'd work out what to do by then. Meanwhile they needed to get home.

They did not approach the former yarn store with caution. And as soon as the old man opened the door he was greeted by Pansy Valiant, who jumped up and licked his face.

Stunned, he made space for his daughter to go in first.

The boy and Mandy sat next to the heater and a candle. They rose.

"You're here!" the old man said.

The old man's daughter ran to her son but he spoke to his grandfather over his mother's shoulder. "I decided we should give you another chance," the boy said. "After all, Grandpa, you're not as young as you used to be and who knows what might happen?"

I've aged ten years today, the old man thought. His daughter just cried with relief onto her son's chest.

Standing back, stroking Pansy Valiant's head, he saw that thin young Mandy was uncertain what to do or say. He opened his arms to the child and she filled them.

As they hugged he thought about the broken latch. There was more to this. The young people – he *mustn't* think of them just as children – the young people had been frightened by *something*. But that was no longer urgent. They were here. They were safe.

As safe as any of them could be in this day and age.

20. DRUGSTORE

The automatic doors whooshed open and the old man walked into a big drugstore.

He wasn't wearing a mask and he had money in his wallet, lots of money. He could feel the wallet's thickness.

He took a shopping cart without wearing gloves. First up, two bottles of wine because he and his wife had friends coming over for dinner. They included his pal Clete from work – because maybe Clete and his wife's cousin Tracy would get along. And if they didn't, so what? They're both nice people and good company, his wife had said. Like their daughter and her husband, the other guests. Six around the table: comfortable.

Maybe three bottles of wine, to be on the safe side, even though their daughter wouldn't drink any because she was pregnant.

All the food was carefully planned of course, including snacks to begin with – his wife never felt easy without a plan. But she did have an odd idea that wine bought ahead wasn't as fresh and tasty as wine bought on the day. He'd often tried to explain what he knew about how wine was made. But she was in charge of the meal so he did it her way.

Or… was she just trying to get him out the house for a couple of hours while she cooked? She always stuck to her story but the kitchen was her domain like the basement workshop was his. That was how things were meant to be, right?

Wine loaded, he came to some artificial flowers. Amazing how genuine plastic flowers could look these days, but his wife preferred real flowers and that's what she would get. Real flowers did have a scent. Would they ever add scent to plastic ones? Maybe they did.

He sniffed some of the plastic lilies. Nope, they only smelled faintly of plastic. But he had to remember to stop at the gas station. He'd get roses there. She deserved roses. He'd fill the tank too. He had the money.

In the next aisle he found children's toys. Was it too early to get toys for the baby? His *grandchild…*

He had no idea whether it would be a boy or a girl and he didn't mind, as long as baby and mother made it through OK. He suspected that his daughter did know the answer to the boy-girl question though she said she didn't. Maybe because her mother didn't want to be told ahead of time. "I want this to be the way it used to be," she'd said. "Do that little thing for me."

"Of course, Ma," their daughter had said. She'd looked at him then, her eyes widening as if he was in on the secret. But a secret that she knew and he didn't? He couldn't remember her telling him but *had* she told him the baby would be a boy? Because when he left the aisle he found he'd put several guns in his cart – even a BB gun like the one his friend Eddie had lent him once.

He shot a pigeon with it. He could *see* the bird now, falling from a telephone wire and then flapping, wounded, in a puddle. He never liked Eddie as much after that.

And now here he was in a drugstore with money in his pocket. As a child he'd never have believed the day would come when he had enough money for what he wanted. Real money. He could buy any tool he felt like and not worry about being followed home.

He set off to choose among the saws and hammers but then found himself taking down a girlie magazine from a top shelf. Before opening it he looked each way along the aisle. Empty… And then… Were there *real* women who looked anything like these pictures?

"Hey, old timer, long time no see."

A short man in a dimpled padded coat greeted him. The old man rapidly closed the magazine and took one about trains to cover it.

"Yeah," he said. "Long time."

"You won't forget we're meeting up tomorrow." It was a statement and the short man grinned, showing sharp teeth.

"Tomorrow," the old man said, nodding. "Sure as shootin'."

"Sure as shootin'," the man in the padded coat said with a nod, and he passed on by.

When he was alone again the old man ditched the trains and put the girlie magazine in his cart. He could hide it under the guns.

He fingered a bulge in a pocket. Was that a handgun? Had he brought one with him?

But if he was meeting the short man he should get a map. They had maps in drugstores.

And then he found himself among beauty products. Hair coloring and eye make-up, nail polish and false nails.

Nails… Yes, nails were good.

But were they on his list? He'd come out with a list, in his wife's clear handwriting. Wine. Flowers…

He checked his pockets but couldn't find it.

Well, you couldn't go wrong with nails. And he had the money.

In the next aisle freezers lined one side. He quickly found bags of ice. You needed ice at a party: wasn't that one of those universal truths? But he didn't remember ice being on the list.

Where was the list? What *was* on it?

Fuck! His wife's prescription! He rushed to the pharmacy counter. There was a line. Not a proper line: people were spaced out six feet apart. Why were they doing that?

But when he pushed past one woman she said, "Hey, wait your turn. And keep your distance."

Something was going on that he didn't understand, but then he was at the front of the line and the dumpy bald pharmacist behind the counter said, "Next."

"I want my wife's prescription," the old man said.

"Name?" the bald man said without interest.

"Whose name?"

"The person the prescription is for. Are you an idiot?"

And he couldn't remember his wife's name. He couldn't *remember* it!

"She'll die without it," he told the pharmacist. "Please, *please*, give me the prescription!"

"Name!"

"I don't know!" he cried. "She'll die! She'll die! She'll die!" He was so powerless. What could he *do*?

Suddenly the old man was aware that his daughter was shaking his shoulders. "Pa? Pa?"

"She'll *die!*" He couldn't bear it. Then, "What? What?"

"You were dreaming, Pa."

"I was?" He looked around. The drab, dim walls of the yarn store. His daughter held a candle. Where was the bright clean drugstore?

"And you were screaming, Pa," his daughter said.

"Was I?" He hadn't gotten his wife's medicine and she *had* died.

"I had to wake you up," his daughter said, yawning. "Are you OK? Do you want a hot drink?"

"I'm fine, love. Thank you," the old man said. "Go back to sleep now."

"If you're sure," she said, returning to her side of the room.

Where she blew out the candle.

The old man was in darkness again. He turned to the wall and hid his face in the shirt he used as a makeshift pillow. And he cried.

21. OLD MAN ON A MISSION

The old man was nervous. He had good reason but that didn't make the feeling any more comfortable. And he worried that his nerves would make him look suspicious if he was stopped.

There was no special reason he should be stopped today, but did Buttons have nervousness detectors along with all the other contraptions they carried?

A pickup passed. It was stacked with timber planks projecting over its back flap. What wouldn't he give for a pile of wooden planks like that, along with a saw, a hammer, nails…

It had been ages since he'd made *anything*. He missed his tools – gone like everything he couldn't carry on his back. So many things had been lost.

He slowed, then stopped, breathing hard. Missing life as it used to be. Missing his wife.

They hadn't realized how good they had it back then. Dissatisfactions and ambitions sometimes undercut the pleasure of having each other and their daughter and, eventually, their grandson; the pleasure of having enough to eat, a place to live, never being cold. And having tools…

But there was no point wallowing. He was on a mission. He began walking again. He had somewhere to go.

"Hey, Old Timer."

Some days it seems like anything that can go wrong, will go wrong.

The old man was shaking. Nerves… He turned. "You mean me?"

The Buttons was no taller than he was but much broader – muscular *and* fat. "Of course I mean you. You see anybody else around here?"

The old man looked one way, then the other and shook his head. Then he stepped toward the Buttons and extended a hand. "How d'ya do?" he said. "Sir."

The Buttons ignored the hand. "What are you up to?"

"Walking, sir. We're supposed to get exercise every day, yeah?"

It had been a long time since the old man had heard any such directive. But he was Old Timer, right?

"You ain't meant to be on the street without you got serious business." The Buttons unclipped the scanner from his belt. "So why *are* you here?"

"Trying to keep alive," the old man said truthfully. "Sir. It's no good if I just sit all day." He held out his ID.

The Buttons scanned the card and waited for the results. They came through quickly. Must be a good reception area. "No fixed abode," he said to the old man.

"Fix me an abode," the old man said. "Please."

"A daughter and a grandson?"

"That's right."

"So where are they?"

"Truth is, I don't know. I'm looking for them. Do you know where they are?"

"I thought you was just walking."

"I am. I only remembered I'm looking for the girl and her boy when you said about them. I knew I'm meant to be doing something. So where are they?"

The Buttons studied the man before him. Slowly he shook his head. "Something about you's not right. Got any weapons?"

The old man laughed. "Damn, I left the rocket launcher at my unfixed abode. But if you scan me, I tell you now, my left armpit will drive your machine crazy."

The Buttons stared at him. Then squinted at the old man's left armpit.

"I had a shoulder replacement back in the day. They put in a chunk of metal where my shoulder bones stopped working. I can only lift my arm this high, even now." He used his right hand to raise his left arm not quite parallel to the ground. "Any higher and it hurts like holy hell. But I can raise my right arm high as you like."

Dropping his left arm he pointed his right hand to the sky high above his head. "Look," he said. "There's a bird up there. You got a gun. If you shoot it, I can cook it. We'll share." The old man pointed two fingers, cocked his thumb and fired. "Bang, bang."

"Put your damn arm down."

"You're right," the old man said, nodding toward his right armpit. "Your machine won't find any metal in there. But I warn you, I ain't had any deodorant to use for years now. Unless you got some? Can I have some of yours? I'm downwind from you and I don't smell a thing. I bet you guys get supplied with all the deodorant you want."

The Buttons flipped a switch on his scanner and passed it half-heartedly over the old man. It screamed when it was near the left armpit but the Buttons seemed more interested in what the old man might have in his pockets. A beep sounded near the right trouser pocket. "What you got in there?"

The old man brought out a long nail. "I found it in the street. It's a little bent but I thought it might come in handy sometime."

The Buttons shook his head. "Get out of here, Old Timer. Go home."

*

Cautiously the old man approached the store where his daughter did her birthday shopping for the boy and Pansy Valiant. It seemed years ago.

At first he looked at the window, seeming to study the displays. In fact he was concentrating on what he could see in the window's reflections.

He was still jumpy. *Was* this going to be a day when everything would go wrong? But he'd done pretty well with the Buttons. Maybe his nerves had turned into an adrenaline rush. Didn't that happen, like when you were lining up for a race and then gun went?

He saw himself reflected in the window, a doddery old guy in makeshift layers of clothing. That wasn't the way he felt though: he was a man on a mission. Let anyone else see whatever they wanted to. There was life in this Old Timer yet.

Then behind his own image he caught a movement. That's what he was looking for. He pivoted and crossed the street. Sure enough, a man was visible in a shadowy doorway. He must be the black-marketeer who'd hailed his daughter.

Not tall, but bundled up in a padded coat suitable for the weather. And perhaps also showing off what he could get for his customers.

As the old man approached, the padded hustler looked one way, then the other. Checking escape routes if the stranger approaching him was hostile?

The old man held out his hands to show they were empty.

The man in the doorway pulled a mask up from around his throat and said, "You want something, pal?"

It was said ambiguously, as if the stranger might be approaching to bum a smoke.

"I hear you're a man who can provide things, if the price is right."

The padded man gave him a shark-like look and raised his eyebrows. "Could be."

"I'm interested in tools," the old man said.

A nod. Then the shark said, "Let's go somewhere a little less public." He led the way to an alley.

The old man tucked his right hand inside his jacket as far as his left armpit. Before following, he looked around but saw no one. He seemed to be alone in the shark-infested water… Deep breath. Here we go.

"You want tools," the shark said when they were out of sight. "You can pay for them?"

"Depends on the price."

"I mean cash in hand. I don't take no barter or shit like that." The shark narrowed his eyes.

"I've got cash hidden away safe." Not to be outdone, the old man narrowed his eyes too.

"Like buried bags of doubloons they used to find with detectors sometimes? Some of them was hid in the craziest places."

"Is that the kind of respect you show paying customers?" The old man shook his head dismissively. "I'm talking paper money. The real thing. Current stuff."

"Where'd you get it?" The shark seemed to be taking him more seriously now.

"I prayed hard," the old man said. "Are you in business or not?"

"Show me some of this real money you got."

The old man pulled a twenty-dollar-bill from the pants pocket that held the nail.

The shark studied both sides. Then took out a blue light and studied it again. "Good. And you got more?"

"If I need more," the old man said, his hand returning to its place under his jacket.

"You got a list?"

The old man produced a list.

"Building something?" the black-marketeer said as he studied it.

"A church to honor my generous god. Can you get it or not?"

"I can get it."

"Everything? Good quality?"

"Everything, and good." The shark rubbed his chin through the mask. "Three days." And he named a figure.

"Give me back the list," the old man said. "You're a mug if you take me for a mug."

"Some of this ain't easy, y'know? Like the crosscut saw."

The old man named a figure. It was a third of what he'd been asked for. They settled on a price a little over half the original number.

"Three days?" the old man asked.

"Three days."

And they agreed how the old man would pick the tools up safely. He put his hand out. The shark extended a hand as if to shake on the deal. "No," the old man said. "I want my twenty back."

"I'll need it to show to the people I deal with."

"Show your own money. You've seen mine and I want it. Now."

Sighing as if he was he was doing the old man a huge favor the shark handed over the note. "This kind of business we got to trust one another."

"I agree," the old man said. "I stick by my deals." He pocketed his twenty and then, from his left armpit, he pulled out a gun.

"Whoa," the black-marketeer said, stepping back. "I ain't carrying *my* money."

"And I don't want your damn money," the old man said. "This goes well and maybe we can do a lot more business. But you need to know it won't be smart to try to screw with me. I've already nearly had to shoot a Buttons today. Shooting you would be nothing."

*

The old man was in a hurry to get home but he still took special care to avoid running into another Buttons. As he walked he thought about how he'd report his encounters to the small family.

"You really said *that*?" his daughter might ask. "Wow."

Yeah, wow, the old man thought. I was pretty good back there. Nerves be damned. That *was* adrenaline. He wanted badly to tell them all about both the men he'd met and how he'd handled the meetings. He also wanted a cup of coffee and to get warm because he was shaking to beat the ban. His jumpiness had well and truly caught up with him. Even if he'd tried, he wouldn't be able to shoot a bird out of the sky *now*.

He wanted to stop to catch his breath but he pushed on. His waiting family would be worried.

It wasn't mission accomplished, yet. But he'd shown that he still had the juice to give his family a chance of escape.

22. WASTE NOT, WANT NOT

"The crowbar again now," the old man said.

His grandson passed him the crowbar and positioned himself to share some of the weight.

"Ready with the hammers."

They'd already done it several times and were getting quicker, more skillful. The old man would bend his knees and put all his weight on the crowbar, prising the end of a floorboard against an underlying joist. The boy would add a little weight, but this was mostly the old man's job.

When the board was up a bit the old man's grandson would slip the claws of both hammers underneath the board on either side. Each would grab a hammer handle to pry the board yet farther, taking turns to move a hammer along until they'd freed the board completely. Often the nails would scream as they were pulled from the joists.

And sometimes a board would snap and one or both men would go flying. But broken boards were good too. They could be used as crosspieces.

Together they'd begun talking to each board as they worked on it. "Come on, y'bastard," the old man might say. "Bastard, c'mon," his grandson might answer. And they would laugh. And grunt. And sweat.

The old man never had a father or grandfather to teach him about tools or wood but his aunt's boyfriend, Charlie, did a certain amount of work around the house. He'd watched and tried to help.

But Charlie had no interest in sharing what he knew. The boy was just about tolerated because it was his auntie's house and, as the old man now recognized, Charlie was mooching off her.

Then one morning Charlie found a possum trapped in the garage. The old man had run out to see it and was there when Charlie smashed the creature's head with a lump hammer. "That's all they deserve," he'd said. "Now clean up the mess." The old man had never watched Charlie work with tools again.

But now, here, working with his grandson gave the old man pleasure. It was hard. Physically the hardest either of them had done in months – for the boy, possibly ever. Even so, after most of a day's work, they'd accumulated a good stock of planks.

Yes, his back hurt but it got some respite after each board came up and they banged nails out it. A hammer each, and starting from opposite ends. It became a game, seeing how few whacks with a hammer each nail took. "Look, grandpa!" "Look, grandson!"

Men's work made into men's play…

In quiet moments man and boy would hear tap-tap tapping from below, as the old man's daughter and Mandy pounded the best of the nails straight.

Flintstone on concrete: like cavewomen pounding grain. Life had galloped backwards in so many ways, the old man thought with a pang. He'd not thought to buy smaller hammers for this task, not thought that the recovered nails might come in handy alongside the new ones he *had* ordered.

The yarn store also now stank of the polyurethane they were using to waterproof the wood. That was modern-ish, wasn't it?

A phrase his wife used to repeat came back to him: "Make do and mend." And "waste not, want not". She'd been old-fashioned that way even when he first met her. He heard them most often when his yearning for new things came close to overcoming him.

But having had a childhood when he almost never owned anything new, sometimes he'd resented her wisdom, even sulked. But it was the same wisdom he was valuing now as he tore up his old home to build something new.

They'd needed wood. After much discussion it was Mandy who'd pointed out the solution: the upstairs room had a wooden floor, unlike the cold concrete underfoot at ground level.

Harder work than buying the wood, but *much* safer than getting it through the black-marketeer. And cheaper.

One transaction with the shark was plenty. The whole procedure of paying for the old man's list of items and getting them home had been filled with steps they couldn't control. Worries about what surprises they'd have to deal with. Who besides the shark might they might have to face. Would they run into a Buttons? Might the whole thing be a trap?

And would Mandy be OK alone in the yarn store?

It was agreed that they'd take three people, two guns and one dog to the pick-up.

Would the shark try to keep the goods and steal the money? That wouldn't happen without a fight.

*

At the appointed time the old man found the black-marketeer in the alley where they'd met before. But once they were out of sight from the street, the old man had again shown his gun.

"Hey, man, hey!" the shark protested. "We're doin' business here."

"I need to be sure that's all we're doing," the old man said.

"What do you take me for?" the man said. "Don't answer that, but yer gettin' shit without I see the money."

The old man showed the money, then tucked it away again. "And you're not getting a dime till I see you've got what I ordered."

"'Course, man. It's not far."

They'd walked together for five minutes.

The old man knew his daughter and her son were following at a safe distance. He concentrated on looking for signs of movement in any of the shadowed places they approached and passed.

He kept his gun aimed at the black-marketeer through the pocket of his coat. And he made sure the man knew that's what he was doing.

*

Everything the old man had ordered was provided. The saw was new and sharp. The two hammers weren't new but they had metal shafts, as specified. The crowbar was fullsize. And the rest: nails, polyurethane, brushes, mineral spirit, nylon rope, zip ties, sharp knife…

Together the little family had managed to get everything back to the yarn store without incident.

They'd talked ahead of time about how they'd handle being stopped by a Buttons.

"We might have to shoot him. Or her," the old man had said. "Are you up to that?"

His daughter hadn't said a definitive yes, but it was understood.

The boy, however, said, "They carry a lot of neat stuff, the Buttons."

"We're not going *hunting*," his mother had said.

"Just saying," he said with a smile.

But no Buttons were harmed in the course of their transaction and they were in a celebratory mood as they clustered around the camp stove when they got home.

Mandy, of course, wanted to know all about it, and the old man was more than happy to share. Everything had gone to plan and, personally, he felt he had done well, again. What a relief, on both counts.

"I talked to him while we walked together," he told everyone.

"We saw that," his daughter said, "but we couldn't hear."

"You know," the old man said. "Just the usual kind of chitchat. Where was he born? How long had he been in this business? Did he have connections who could get us to Canada."

They smiled and chuckled, responding to the lightness in his voice.

"What did your new buddy say about Canada, Pa?" his daughter asked.

"He might be able to set that up but it would cost a hell of a lot more than I paid him today. And it would depend how many people I wanted to move. I told him there'd be eleven adults, three children and a dog."

"Are you the Pied Piper now?" his daughter said.

"He needed to know there were too many of us to mess with. And he might have spotted Pansy Valiant already."

"And what did he say?" the boy asked.

"That he'd check around and I should get back to him in a few days. I knew where to find him."

"I bet he spotted Pansy Valiant." The boy pulled the dog closer. "That's why none of his pals jumped you."

"You've hit the brand new nails on the head there," the old man said. "Is the coffee ready?"

It was. Everyone had a cup. They clinked them in a toast to their success.

Then Mandy raised a hand. "Sir?"

The old man was shocked momentarily by the formality. Almost everything she did and said seemed to tell them more about her upbringing. "Love?"

"Where's Canada?"

Gently he said, "It's a place up north. A good place. But we're not going there – it's not warm enough."

"Oh!" she said. "You lied?"

"I misdirected," the old man said looking from her to his daughter to his grandson to Pansy Valiant.

Mandy said nothing, but he thought she was beginning to understand about lies and safety because then she lifted her coffee and said, "To lovely warm Canada."

Everyone laughed. It was Mandy's first joke. She was, the old man thought, beginning to feel like she was part of the family.

23. WARMTH

"There's one good thing about winter, Pa…"

"Oh yeah?" the old man said eventually, all but unable to move. It seemed that every muscle he owned now ached from his exertions over recent days. He'd never felt anything like it before.

But neither he nor any of them had ever done anything like this before.

"In the winter," his daughter went on, "the nights are longer." She paused, giving him a chance to respond. Then she laughed. "More darkness? You're short a few cents on the dollar tonight, aren't you?"

"Excuse me if I don't dance a jig," the old man finally said. He sorely regretted not ordering painkillers from the black-marketeer. Sorely… But he didn't have the energy to share this thought. The aspirins in the first aid kit were long gone.

"C'mon, Pa. We're on our way, at last!"

And they were. No denying that. They were floating down the river on a raft. A raft they'd made together from the destruction of their last home.

"I can't see lights from the city anymore," the old man's daughter said, her excitement evident. "Whatever happens from here, *they* won't be getting us."

"That's true," the old man mustered. He and his family had taken their fates into their own hands. Something in the future might get them, but at least it wouldn't be Buttons looking for Mandy, Buttons with meatloaf lures, or Buttons making them kneel down and empty their backpacks.

Would there be Buttons downriver? There was bound to be some kind of law enforcement. If not Buttons then… Stripes? Or Stars?

Where did *that* come from? he wondered. The stars and stripes didn't mean a whole lot these days. There was precious little evidence of federal governing now.

At some point they'd float into the waters of a new state. Were there waterway "Welcome to…" signs like those posted at borders on the interstates?

He and his wife had taken their girl on the interstates, just the once. They wanted her to see the ocean. It was only for a weekend but they'd been lucky with the weather: hot, sunny, genuinely summery.

They'd been less lucky with the motel, but it was all they could afford even though both he and his wife had jobs. However seeing the girl explore the incoming waves as they washed over her feet, watching her run back and forth giggling, flushed with sun and excitement… A truly happy time. Not even the roaches could ruin it. It had been worth all the scrimping and saving.

The old man and his wife had waded in the surf where the water was warm.

"Do you remember seeing the ocean?" the old man asked.

"What, Pa?"

"The ocean. Do you—"

"It tickled my feet!" she said. "And I saw little fishies!"

He didn't know about little fishes in the river but now she could dangle her feet in the water whenever she wanted. Though he'd been splashed a lot as they'd launched themselves and the river was cold in the dark. So maybe later. Warmth was what they were aiming for with *this* trip.

"I think I've got one," his grandson called from the end of the raft.

"End"? There had to be a fancier word. The stern? Could rafts have sterns? Better than calling it the "butt," he supposed.

Mandy was taking a turn as the lookout at the front. They needed to be alert for obstacles like rocks or fallen trees or rubbish like that which clogged the river as it ran through the city. Potentially more dangerous were other boats, which would probably show lights.

Theirs was a dark vessel. If they saw a light coming toward them or overtaking them the plan was to steer for the nearest available bit of shore. Steering wasn't easy, but they could do it. And they'd decided it would be safest if they moved by night, at least to begin with.

There was a splash from the back. "Ah shit," the boy said. "It got away."

He was fishing while also making sure the tiny second raft stayed close behind the main raft and didn't get snagged on something.

They'd had leftover wood. Waste not, want not… So with one raft completed, they built a second and tied a few supplies to it. Later maybe they'd want to use it as a flat-bottomed canoe. Who knew what would come in handy downriver.

Their whole lives were afloat…

But they did have paddles, two of them. *And* their stores included an inflatable raft – OK, it was the kind that children used to play with in swimming pools, but better than nothing. Just about their last task "ashore" had been to go on a spending spree.

The old man's daughter went to the camping store they'd robbed long ago. She bought gas canisters, plastic sheeting, more zip ties, fishing tackle, water-wings… Her son could swim but Mandy couldn't.

The old man had waited outside in case of trouble.

With one of the guns. Like old times.

And if the money she'd used was traceable it no longer mattered. They'd be gone – slipping away on a slow current.

Their vessel had surprisingly few straight lines or right angles. But she did the job and the old man was proud of her. Should the raft have a name? The Doris?

His wife's name, it meant "bountiful" and was originally the name of a Greek water nymph. She'd looked it up.

"How are you feeling, Pa?"

"The better for being able to lie down at last."

"It's cold though."

"Bracing. Don't jerks somewhere call it bracing?"

She laughed. Then, "Do you know what day it is?"

"Independence day?"

"The day that predatory Buttons was expecting to have me for dinner."

"He won't like that you stood him up. Should we have put our launch off?" He coughed. "Meatloaf, you know…"

"It was either stand him up or kill him, and we only have so many bullets."

"Hah."

The old man's daughter had already shot one Buttons that day. Shot, but not killed. He knew she was still shaky about it.

They'd been intercepted by a Buttons on their last trip from the old yarn store to the river. There'd been no explanation they could give about what they were up to, loaded with so many things. "Where are you going? What do you think you're doing? Empty those bags." So the old man's daughter fired at the Buttons' scanner.

It shattered and flew out of the big woman's hand. Her hand wasn't hurt but a shard of plastic hit the woman's face. She screamed and covered her eyes.

Using the Buttons' own cuffs the old man pinned her hands behind her back before cutting a strip off her shirt to cover the wound. Then he'd secured her feet with her belt. "She'll live," he said.

"You two are dead meat," the Buttons growled.

If she could still threaten them she couldn't be too badly hurt, he thought. He stuffed one her gloves in her mouth and together the old man and his daughter dragged the Buttons off the sidewalk and into a dark gap between buildings.

"We need to get back up the hill. We're late," his daughter had said before they left the immobilized woman.

It was intended to mislead, of course.

They'd hoped to get away without any violence but they couldn't afford to be identified or slowed down. Not this day.

"I never shot anyone before," his daughter said, breaking the silence as they carried their loads back to where the boy and Mandy guarded the raft, with the other gun. Her voice shook.

"When it's them or us," the old man said, "I choose us. It was the only thing you could do."

She nodded, but it was not a nice leave-taking from the city of her birth, of her childhood, of her whole life.

And the encounter made them both fear that there had been trouble at the river launch spot. They were so close…

But Pansy Valiant ran to greet them as they approached. And now they were *gone,* on the river. Heading *south.* Floating away from winter in the city, toward an unknown that must, eventually, at least be warmer.

Poor Mandy. She'd had her first morning sickness.

At the same time they were leaving their old life, the old man thought, a new life was on its way in more ways than one.

Although it was a cold night, the sky was clear and the weather dry. That was one bit of good fortune.

What would they encounter on their way? Storms? Patrol boats? Was there a Coast Guard on rivers? Or pirates? The old man had read about pirates when he was young. He doubted any that they met would fit the fictional stereotype but did the scavengers of the cities also scour the river?

The old man laughed although it hurt his back.

"What's funny, Pa?"

"Just wondering what we're going to meet out here."

Everything was new and uncertain. How and when would they tie up ashore? At some point should they try carrying on in daylight? Would that attract attention – and if so would it be hostile or friendly?

And was the world farther south better, or just as fucked up as the world they'd left?

Well, all the answers would come. Day by day. Hour by hour. Minute by minute.

Was it already feeling a little warmer? the old man wondered. Could he really be feeling that?

He could, because the deepest warmth of his life was being with his daughter and his grandson.

"I caught one!" the boy called again. "For real this time. Fish for breakfast, anyone?"

ABOUT THE AUTHOR

Michael Z. Lewin is an award-winning novelist and short story writer. He first came to the attention of the mystery world with his Indianapolis-set series about private detective, Albert Samson. Indy policeman Leroy Powder soon followed. Mike has also written stand-alone mysteries set in Indiana, where he grew up, as well as a series of novels and stories set in Bath, England, where he lives now. The Bath works follow the adventures of a detective agency run as a family business. Other books include a novel narrated by God, and a short story collection narrated by a stray dog. In 2021 he was given "The Eye", the life achievement award of The Private Eye Writers of America. His work, including some of thirteen radio dramas written for the BBC, has been widely translated.

After graduating high school in Indianapolis Mike moved to New York when he was eighteen. A decade later he moved even farther east to England. More information about his life and *oeuvre* can be found at www.MichaelZLewin.com. He has a presence on Facebook as Michael Z Lewin but is not very active there.

Lightning Source UK Ltd.
Milton Keynes UK
UKHW011535140122
397147UK00001B/29